No Drama

Meg Franco

First published by Dog Ear Publishing
4010 W. 86th Street, Ste H
Indianapolis, IN 46268
www.dogearpublishing.net

ISBN: 978-1-4575-1949-9

This book is printed on acid-free paper.

This book is a work of fiction. Places, events, and situations in this book
are purely fictional and any resemblance to actual persons, living or dead,
is coincidental.

Printed in the United States of America

*K*elly woke up to the sound of shouting. Her mother and father were screaming at each other again. Kelly knew there would be trouble when he didn't show up for dinner. The yelling got louder and Kelly covered her head with her comforter. It was an odd word for a blanket, comforter. She didn't feel very comforted right now.

Kelly glanced over at her sister Peggy. Peggy was pretending to be asleep, but Kelly knew she was faking it by the way her eyes were squeezed shut. Kelly knew her parents loved each other. Her father was just "too much" as her mother had been known to say. Kelly agreed. She loved her Dad, but it was always something. He didn't show up when he was supposed to, he spent money they didn't have. Who cared if he bought them an expensive trampoline when the result was no electricity for ten days because they didn't have money to pay the bill? Eating a cold dinner by candle light was fun the first night, but by the third night it got really old.

The yelling continued and Kelly rolled over, stuck her fingers in her ears and squeezed her eyes shut in an exact replica of her sister. When I grow up, I will never fight with my husband. He won't do this to me. I never want to love someone so much that they can make me yell and cry, never.

Kelly waited until the shouting moved down the hall and away from the bedrooms. She quietly slipped out of bed and inched herself over to her bedroom window. She eased it open as softly as she could, glancing over to see if she'd woken Peggy up. Sometimes Peggy would come with her, but tonight Kelly just wanted to escape by her-self.

She climbed over the window ledge and grabbed onto the huge pine tree that was three feet away. Kelly climbed down silently, taking her time, not bothering to use the flashlight she always carried with her on these nocturnal journeys in case of an emergency or strange and frighten-ing noises. The moon was huge and white in the sky mak-ing it very easy to navigate through the woods to Jay's house.

Kelly hid in the azalea bushes and threw pebbles at his window until his sleepy face appeared in the moonlight. It disappeared again and fifteen long minutes later Jay appeared on the first floor, sneaking out the kitchen door with a brown paper bag under his arm.

They walked silently back through the woods until they came to the tree house they had built together, with the help of their fathers. It was relatively large for a tree house and they unrolled their sleeping bags and laid side by side in silence.

Jay knew the drill, Kelly would spill the beans when she was ready.

"Why does she always have to fight with him, Jay? Why can't my mom just be happy he's home and get over it?"

Jay shrugged, "Maybe she just wants to be enough. Maybe she's tired of him not being around."

Jay had heard his parents talking from time to time about Kelly's mom. Poor Poppy, they called her. Jay's mom said she'd never put up with Patrick's shenanigans, but his father pointed out that Poppy had no family, no income, where could the poor woman go?

Kelly stared at Jay, knowing there was something he wasn't telling her, afraid to even hear what it might be.

"When I grow up I just want someone easy. I don't want to fight or deal with the drama, Jay. I'm not going to care if he goes out or misses dinners. As long as he doesn't make me yell and cry, I'll be happy. I don't want to be in love. It's too hard."

Jay stared at Kelly, watching as a fat tear rolled down her cheek and pooled at the tip of her nose before dropping onto her sleeping bag.

"Don't worry Kelly. No one can make you fall in love. You have to be ready for it. It'll happen when you're ready. Pass the brown bag. I stole my dad's lighter and a bag of marshmallows. Let the feast begin."

They toasted marshmallows on sticks, taking turns with the pilfered lighter until they couldn't eat any more.

Kelly snuggled into her sleeping bag and reached for Jay's hand. "You're my best friend Jay. Don't let your brothers stop you from being my friend, ok?"

Jay laughed. "Please, Kelly, as long as I stay away from them they're happy. Just promise me you won't marry one of them. That would really suck. In fact, don't marry anyone I don't like, promise?"

Kelly smiled. "You like everyone except your brothers, so that leaves me a lot of boys to choose from. No problem."

Kelly rolled over and went to sleep. Jay tried to stay awake to watch the sunrise, but he was softly snoring within five minutes of Kelly, too tired to even get under his blanket.

Chapter 1

*K*elly Chambers never thought her marriage would end and certainly not because her husband joined a gym. Matt had started working out to "relieve stress." Then he kept working out because he looked so good. Pretty soon he was at the gym more than he was home.

In retrospect Kelly realized she should have suspected something, but in all honesty she was relieved to have the time to herself. It didn't even occur to her to be suspicious. When all was said and done Kelly guessed she just didn't love him enough to be jealous. Matt wasn't her best friend. He'd become the annoying human being she happened to co exist with. The person whose socks she was forced to pick up. He was the roommate who would ask if she stopped for groceries when she walked in the door instead of asking before she got home or, God forbid, getting them himself. He was like an annoying child she was forced to look after. Kelly could remember loving him, but she couldn't quite dredge up the feeling more than once or twice a year.

Still, Kelly couldn't get over the fact that he left her for the girl who checks ID's at the front desk of the gym. It turns out that Debbie was twenty three, but at the time Kelly thought she was in high school. Debbie wasn't gorgeous, she didn't appear smart. There was nothing about

1

her that screamed "home wrecker." Kelly is five foot six inches, a little curvy, not fat, with brown hair and blue eyes. She was no Cindy Crawford or Kate Moss, but she was definitely better looking than Debbie.

The day she found out Matt was cheating was a banner day. She woke up late and had to rush into work. Kelly was the owner of "In Disguise", a very seasonal, fun store. They specialized in all types of costumes and Kelly had developed a huge internet base, often renting the costumes to movie production companies. Fun, but not very profitable, unfortunately. Still, it paid the bills.

It was the end of September so business was just starting to pick up. The air was cool and crisp. It was a perfect fall day. Kelly almost cracked her car up checking out the beautiful reds, oranges and golds of the fall foliage. She had left Matt a note saying she would meet him at the gym when the store closed for the day. Kelly did this about twice a month. She preferred yoga or Pilates or a good long walk with her boxer, Max. As it turned out, Matt didn't see the note.

After selling 20 Hannah Montana costumes and measuring a particularly large and annoying man for a King Arthur costume, Kelly was actually happy to be heading to the gym. She parked her car next to Matt's truck and grabbed her gym bag from the back seat and headed inside.

The temperature had cooled down a lot since she went into work that morning and it felt great. Kelly loved everything about the fall; the crisp mornings, the scent of the falling leaves, the burning log smell from nearby chimneys. She always imagined the cheerful, crackling fires from her childhood. She felt energized and happy. She'd do a quick circuit and head to the market to pick up some steaks to throw on the grill for dinner tonight. She had a really great bottle of Pinot Noir and some olives she'd been marinating for a couple of weeks. She'd stop at Rockland Bakery in Nanuet and pick up some crusty bread to round out the meal and they'd be all set. Not that Matt would touch a carb these days, but she'd just have to eat his share.

All these thoughts came to an abrupt end as the gym doors closed behind Kelly with a click. There was her Matt playing with Debbie the ID girl's hair over the counter. Debbie had her back to Matt with her head tilted backwards so it rested on his chest and he was twisting it into a bun on the top of her head while he kissed her neck.

Later she remembered thinking, "wow, that guy looks a lot like Matt", followed swiftly with, "shit, that is Matt". Kelly turned around to walk out but not before Debbie spotted her and let out a squeak alerting Matt. Kelly ran to her car and had just gotten it started when Matt reached her window. Kelly had thought about keying his car or letting the air out of his tires, but since the truck was in her name it seemed a bit silly. She really wished she had a stun gun or brass knuckles. Boy would Matt be in for a shock when she rolled her window down. Well at least he'd save on the dental floss bill if she managed to get in a good enough shot. Kelly was laughing to herself as she lowered her window. Whatever Matt was expecting her reaction to be laughter wasn't it. He regarded her cautiously.

"Kelly, it's not what it looks like. I was planning on talking to you as soon as

I got things straight in my head. Debbie and I just hit it off. We really like each other. We have a lot in common. She really gets me Kelly."

Kelly snorted. "I can't believe you just said that, Matt, and it's clearly exactly what it looks like, jackass."

Matt stood up angrily and stepped back from Kelly's car. "You know we haven't gotten along for years now, Kelly. How did you think this was going to play out?"

Kelly just stared at Matt. "I don't know Matt. I guess I never thought about it playing out one way or the other. I thought at the very least we'd walk away friends. I guess you have to be friends in the first place to be able to walk away as friends. I need to leave Matt."

Kelly backed out quickly before Matt could formulate another half assed thought. In the process she almost ran Matt's best friend Nick over. He'd been standing behind the car listening, but Kelly was too engrossed in her conversation with Matt to even notice him. Too bad it wasn't Matt, thought Kelly. She would have been doing humanity a favor if she ran him over. Maybe even be rewarded with a Nobel peace prize. Oh well, thank God Nicky was nothing if not quick on his feet.

So Nicky knew too. No surprise there. He probably set them up. They'd been best friends since they were five when Matt's family moved in next door. They played baseball and football together. The only season they weren't attached at the hip was during the winter when Nicky wrestled and Matt played basketball.

Still, in recent years their friendship had seemed to die down a bit. They still ran into each other at friend's parties and at the gym, but they didn't seem to enjoy it. They would exchange pleasantries and head in different directions as quickly as possible. Kelly had tried to grill Matt about it, but he would get defensive and blame it on Nick being a pretentious asshole. Kelly never really bought that story. Nick could be a pain in the ass at times, but he'd never been anything but down to earth.

Chapter 2

_K_elly met Nick Flynn on her first day at campus at SUNY Oneonta. She thought he was hot. He was about 5'11" with black hair and grey eyes fringed with thick, black eyelashes only girls should have. Plus, he was really nice. At first, that is.

They were stuck on line together for two hours waiting to register for their fall classes. They discovered they both liked the Beatles, red meat and Twix bars. And they were both from Rockland County, New York, although Kelly had gone to Pearl River High school and Nick had attended Don Bosco, an all boys' school. Kelly was in serious lust. So of course there had to be a catch.

Enter the girl friend. Trish was very pretty in a skinny, blond, anemic way. She was the kind of girl that men feel the need to help all the time. She had a little girl voice to boot. Give me a break, Kelly thought. She almost rolled her eyes the first time Trish opened her mouth and spoke. Nick didn't look particularly happy to see her. Nick and Kelly ended up in two classes together. She was really psyched about it, Trish or no Trish. Not surprisingly, Trish looked less then thrilled. She looked even less excited when Nick invited Kelly back to his dorm that night for a party. She was trying to look friendly and glare at the same time which really was a very unappealing look for her.

Kelly took a lot of time dressing that night. She borrowed a soft white sweater with rhinestone buttons from her new roommate Angie who was extremely weird, but very nice. Angie was five feet tall with white blond hair and yellow eyes. The night before she caught Kelly trying to count how many earrings she had and blurted "eighteen!" If she weighed 100 pounds it was soaking wet and wearing all of her clothes. She only had one tattoo that was visible on her ankle and it said "meow". Kelly begged Angie to go to the party so she wouldn't have to walk in alone.

They arrived at 11pm because Kelly didn't want to look too eager. After a couple of minutes she saw Nick across the room. He was busy helping another guy hold some girl upside down over the keg while she drank from the tap. Angie said "this sucks, I'm out of here" and left so quickly that Kelly didn't have time to beg her to stay. Angie explained to Kelly later that night that she doesn't drink very often because when she does drink, it usually ends unpleasantly. She can get very nasty, all five feet of her.

Nick spotted Kelly and his face lit up. He made his way across the room to her just as Tricia came running up dragging someone in tow. "Here's the girl I've been telling you about Matt."

It wasn't love at first sight. Matt was tall and stocky with blondish brown hair and brown eyes. He looked like he got dressed in the dark, but he was very friendly. They hit it off right away in an easy carefree kind of way. No sparks. Kelly didn't feel the excitement and connection she'd felt with Nick, but Matt was definitely appealing. She remembered thinking that it was probably a good thing not to feel that fission of excitement, safer.

Kelly spent the majority of the next four years with Matt or Angie. Angie didn't really like Matt all that much, but she got along great with Nick, which made life easier. Even though Angie and Nick never became more than friends, they would often do things as a foursome. Nick was always in between girlfriends and most guys were scared of Angie.

After Kelly started dating Matt, Nick seemed to distance himself. He almost seemed to hate Kelly most of the time. He broke up with Tricia before the Christmas break freshman year and proceeded to sleep his way through the female population for the next three and a half years. When they graduated Matt and Kelly went back to Rockland and moved in together. They got married six months later.

They said they'd talk about children in four years, but now they were both thirty three and the closest Kelly came to children was at the costume store and her nephew Sam. There always seemed to be a reason to put it off, mortgage payments, work commitments, etc. They borrowed Sam on a regular basis and gave him back when they were tired. Kelly's sister Peggy works sixty hours a week for "Canada Dry" and her husband Tim works in management for Verizon and his home office is in Colorado. He worked from home when he could manage it, but he sometimes had to bite the bullet and go in to the home office.

Kelly ended up taking Sam to football and baseball practice ninety percent of the time. "Aunt Kelly, can you put the pads in my football pants? Aunt Kelly, I need more water." Kelly had always felt like she had a child. And Sam enjoyed having two moms. Some of the football parents had thought Kelly and Peggy were a couple at first. When he was 4 years old Sam told Kelly she shouldn't have children because they might be Vampires and did she really want to have to stake her own children?

Kelly arrived home that night from the gym and started packing. Matt made the money and she couldn't afford the mortgage. Hopefully he'd buy her out without a hassle. It never occurred to her to try and work it out. She was done. No kids, no foul, except for the dog, and Matt hated Max. She loaded her things into her blue 2000 Acura and figured she'd come back for the rest.

"What do you mean you moved out?" Peggy glared at Kelly. You never leave the marital residence, never! Did you even try and talk to Matt?"

Peggy had inherited the temper. Kelly tried to explain that she just didn't care anymore. She just had no more energy to waste on trying to fix something she didn't break. Peggy listened impatiently and after glaring at Kelly a little longer gestured to the couch.

"Well, I guess you can sleep there until you figure this out."

Peggy stomped out of the room. Gee whiz, Peg, thanks so much thought

Kelly.

Sam came bounding into the room, wooden sword in hand. "To the death, Aunt Kelly!"

Kelly put her hands up to protect her face. "Not to the death, Sam! The last time we had a sword fight it took three weeks for my pinky finger to recover. I really don't feel too great right now, Sammy. Maybe later, ok?" Peggy walked back into the room and turned to face Sam.

"You'll be seeing even more of Aunt Kelly than ever, Sam. Aunt Kelly left Uncle Matt and will be residing on our couch for the foreseeable future."

Sam looked at his mother with concern. "Does this mean she won't be giving me cousins with Uncle Matt?"

"Yes honey, she's very selfish. But look at the bright side Sammy. You won't have to share Aunt Kelly and you get to live with that elephant she calls a dog," Peggy said pointing to Max and shuddering. Max put his head on his paws and whined. Max and Peggy had a tenuous relationship at best. Peggy hated him and Max loved her.

"Go outside until football and take Maxi pad with you," Peggy barked at Sam.

Max followed Sam out the back door happily and Kelly waited until she heard the click of the latch before rounding on Peggy.

"Stop telling Sam stupid things, Peggy! This is not my fault!"

Peggy rolled her eyes. "Whatever you say, Kelly," I have a conference call in five minutes. Sam's football crap is in the hallway and I left money for Pizza Hut afterwards. Just think about what you're doing before you make a huge mistake." Peggy glared at Kelly and started to walk up the staircase.

"I wasn't doing anything or anyone. You're lecturing the wrong person."

Peggy continued walking up the stairs. Shaking her head, she stalked into her office and slammed the door.

Peggy kicked off her shoes and walked across the thick, luxurious carpet to her home computer and sat down in her eight hundred dollar office chair with a sigh. She knew this was coming, knew that Matt had been cheating for years. She just kept hoping that Kelly would get pregnant and Matt would get it together and settle down. At least when Matt was home, he would help around the house and handle any necessary repairs, unlike Tim who did nothing when he was around. Peggy was starting to really resent Tim's lack of family participation. She felt like she was never home to begin with and when she was, she was so busy catching up on housework that she didn't get any quality time with Sam. These days, it felt like Kelly was more of a mother to Sam than she was. The money she earned was terrific, but the price she was paying emotionally was too high. She was losing her son and her husband was turning into a stranger. This wasn't where she thought she would be at this stage in the game. They needed to spend more time with Sam, get more involved.

She scrolled through her emails. There was an invitation for a showing of the Nutcracker by the Coupe Dance Studio for December fourth. The proceeds would go towards Rockland food shelters. Great, Peggy thought. She'd buy two tickets for herself and Sam and they'd make a day out of it. The next email was from Sam's little league coach. He was moving and needed to find a replacement coach for this spring. Peggy volunteered Tim for the job. She typed in Tim's cell phone number and email address. Perfect, this was just what they needed to do to be more involved in Sam's life and since she was the house servant, Tim was going to have to take one for the team. How bad could it be?

Chapter 3

*K*elly pulled into the parking lot five minutes late for football practice. She shoved the last of Sam's pads in and he ran onto the field furious that Aunt Kelly had stopped for coffee, making him late and forcing him to run laps as punishment. Sam had already informed her that he was not getting her a Christmas gift as punishment. "Fine by me, Sam," Kelly had replied. Then she'd asked him to pass her the lipstick rolling around in her handbag. Sam dug around and passed it over with a glare after taking off the cap. "Thanks Sammy. I'll try and drive faster, ok?"

"Fine by me, Aunt Kelly" Sam replied with a smirk.

Kelly got her chair and a book out of the Acura's trunk and headed down to the field to join the other parents.

As Sam had suspected would be the case, he was running laps. It must be hard to run laps and glare at someone, but boy was Sam doing a good job thought Kelly as he once again looked over his shoulder at her.

"Keep it up and your face will freeze that way buddy," Kelly yelled.

She opened her chair and put it down in the grass next to Judy. Judy was very loud, Spanish and from the South Bronx originally. Judy thought most of the other mothers were idiots and would only talk to Kelly and Carry

Prescott. Carry wished she didn't. Kelly found Judy very entertaining most of the time. Not tonight.

"What the hell are you wearing Kelly," Judy bellowed. "What are you doing, going Goth?"

Kelly looked down at her leggings and oversized Henley to see if maybe she'd put her underwear on outside of her pants. Nope. "What are you talking about Judy?"

Laughing, Judy pulled out a compact from her oversized bag and handed it to her.

Oh shit thought Kelly. My lips are black. Sam had handed her football black instead of lipstick. "You better keep running Sam!" Sam looked over smiling and pumping his fists in the air. Judy handed Kelly a tissue laughing.

"I was a little jealous that you could put lipstick on without looking in a mirror. Not so much right now," Judy laughed.

Kelly took a long pull on her coffee and held it up in the air. "We'll be stopping for coffee all week long Sam so get used to running laps!"

Sam stopped smiling and put his helmet on so he could mumble in privacy.

Sam plays football for Pop Warner on the Mighty Mites team. The head coach as luck would have it was Nick. Nick loves Sam. He'd been grooming him for two years to be middle linebacker and running back. He took coaching very seriously. At least he'll be too busy to talk to me Kelly thought. No such luck, Nick was heading her way. Time to walk the track Kelly thought, running towards the junior high track. Phew, I dodged that bullet Kelly thought with relief. No such luck.

"Kelly, can we talk for a minute?"

Kelly turned with a sigh. "I'm really not up for this, Nick. Can it wait?"

Nick walked closer and hugged Kelly.

"Well if you need anything or I can help just call my cell phone. I'm your friend too, ok?"

Kelly stared at Nick, flabbergasted. They were friends? Ok, if you say so, wacko, Kelly thought. Still, she felt oddly touched.

"Thanks Nick. Since you mention it, it would be great if you could tell Sam he ran enough laps and get off his ass for the rest of the day."

Nick laughed. "No, but if you need money or a shoulder to cry on, I'm your man, Kells!" Nick smiled, laughed at Kelly's expression and jogged back to the practice field.

Kelly walked around the track for half an hour and then headed back to her folding chair. Sam trotted over and grabbed his water bottle. Giving Kelly a final glare he turned to run back to the field, tripped over her pocketbook and then got up. Head held high he jogged back to his friends refusing to look back at his aunt.

That night Kelly had a bad dream. She was running around the track naked and Matt and Debbie were waving to her. Her family was there and they were yelling and pointing at Debbie. She couldn't hear what they were saying. Kelly was holding a baby but when she looked down at her arms, they were empty. She looked up terrified. Debbie was holding the baby now. Kelly woke up abruptly feeling like someone had died.

Chapter 4

*I*t was a beautiful Indian summer morning. The sun was just making an appearance and it was crisp and cool out. No one was up yet and Kelly had the kitchen to herself. It was her favorite time of the day. Kelly made a pot of coffee and poured herself a huge mug with loads of milk and sugar. Then she made pancakes for Sam and left them far back on the counter out of Max's reach. After a long, hot, leisurely shower Kelly sat with yet another cup of overly sugared coffee and took stock of the day ahead.

The costume store was closed, Sam had no football game and Kelly had no commitments. She put on her oldest, most comfortable jeans and Matt's navy blue cashmere sweater which had accidently on purpose found its way into her suitcase. Kelly ran a brush through her out of control hair and applied mascara and lip gloss. She looked in the mirror and stared at herself. Not too bad Kelly decided. She grabbed her car keys and pocketbook and headed out the door with Max in tow.

Octoberfest was in full swing at Bear Mountain. Kelly called Jay, who said he'd meet her there in an hour. Kelly drove the 20 miles, admiring the beautiful kaleidoscope of fall scenery on the way down the Palisades Parkway. She put Max's leash on and walked him around Hessian Lake three times before collapsing on a bench. Max had run into the water trying to drag Kelly with him, barking at things Kelly couldn't see. I wonder if he's barking at the ghosts of Hessian soldiers, Kelly mused. Her phone beeped with a text message from Jay saying he'd be there in two minutes so Kelly headed back to the front of the Inn where they'd agreed to meet.

Jay came running up impeccably dressed with a vibrant red scarf looped around his neck. "Hello my precious," he said in his best Lord of the Rings voice. He dragged Kelly to the beer stand and got two brimming solo cups of Octoberfest beer and a plate of sauerbraten. They headed to a picnic table with a view of the lake to enjoy their feast.

Jay was positively gleeful about Kelly and Matt's breakup and wasn't remotely trying to hide it. "Ding dong the dick is dead, the dick is dead! Yay!"

Jay was straight, but you would swear he was gay.

He was 6'1" with a slight build. Jay had beautiful features and longish blond hair. He was pretty, rather then handsome. He modeled for local retailers and some national department stores, but his main day job was as a gossip columnist for a local internet paper. It had gotten him in quite a few scrapes over the past couple of years and Kelly was constantly telling him to please not write about her or their friends when it was a slow news day. Sam had made the paper quite a few times also, much to his delight.

Jay had his own checkered dating history. In fact, most of Jay's girlfriends from the past had come out of the closet. Jay loved really masculine looking women who enjoyed bossing him around. If he could only find one who was straight he'd be all set. Kelly kept telling him to stay away from any females who were softball players but he wouldn't listen.

Jay continued to chortle to himself until Kelly asked him to please knock it off.   "I'm sorry, Kelly, but you know I hate him. He's a tool."

Jay pulled Kelly in for a big bear hug and then they sat and drank their beer companionably, just enjoying the beautiful fall colors and scents.

Kelly and Jay had grown up together in a small cul-de-sac backed by miles of forest. They would sneak out of their houses all summer long to play in the woods. Together, and with a little help from Kelly's father, they built a beautiful tree house with wood their families contributed and some that Kelly and Jay pilfered from the many construction sites all over Rockland County. The tree house even had two windows. They kept extra clothes there as well as sleeping bags and snacks. When they got soaked from playing in the stream there was no need to go home and change. They would put on their spare clothes and hang the wet ones out to dry. Neither Kelly nor Jay liked to go home much. Kelly's family was better, but you could never tell when her parents would be fighting over her father's latest transgression.

Jay came from a family of steel workers who really didn't know what to make of him. Even his mother was very manly, though she loved Jay with all her heart. She just didn't know what to do with her less than masculine son. Jay's two brothers were big, brawny football players. Their baby brother was tolerated, but at arm's length and with much eye rolling. They had all assumed he was gay until Jay was a senior in high school and had started to date.

Jay was heartbroken when Kelly met Matt. Matt was not someone Jay wanted to be friends with and Matt hated Jay in return and Jay knew it. It didn't impact Kelly and Jay's friendship but it made life difficult for Kelly at times.

Jay would sit too close to Matt and make a lot of eye contact. He would talk loudly about the mani pedi he just had when Matt was in the room. He would bring over quiche and talk about his and Kelly's girl's night out. He loved to push Matt's buttons. In turn Matt would call Jay "Janie girl" and invite him to football games and guys night out and then try and set him up with the nearest gay man in the vicinity. Passive aggressive dislike at its best. They laughed too hard at each other's jokes and then rolled their eyes at Kelly when the other had his back turned.

"So what's the deal now? High priced lawyers or amicable dividing of the assets? He keeps the gym slut and you get the house, right?"

Kelly looked at Jay and thought there were times she loved him so much it hurt. "We haven't talked about it yet, but Matt pays most of the mortgage so if he buys me out with a fair number I'll be happy. Eventually."

Jay stared at Kelly and started to laugh. "You know, I think you're going to be just fine, eventually. Now let's get another pint and some dessert."

After Bear Mountain they went back to Jay's townhouse and watched the Hangover (Kelly's choice) and Love Actually (Jay's choice), drank martinis and ate White castle hamburgers until they passed out on the leather sectional.

Jay pulled a down comforter over Kelly at about 2am and shut out the lights. Max followed Jay into his room, hopped up on the bed, and made himself comfortable. Jay sighed. Looks like I'll be washing the blankets tomorrow morning.

One more item of business, before I sleep Jay thought, logging into his blog. He typed it in quickly, not wanting to alert Kelly to what he was up to.

"What local philanderer, masquerading as a good guy, is finally getting his just desserts, and all because of a gym tart? Well, all this guy can say is thank you tiny trollop for taking his costume off and exposing Mr. Fraud."

Kelly woke up at 6am hung over and depressed. She folded up Jay's comforter and got her bag, keys and Max and drove home. She went to sleep on the couch with the comforter pulled over her head. The thought of dividing their belongings and packing up made Kelly so depressed all she could do was cry.

Sam padded into the room and climbed under the comforter and lay across Kelly. Sam didn't believe in personal space. "I'm sorry Aunt Kelly. Is your heart broken? I really didn't want cousins anyway, so it's probably good you fired Uncle Matt. Dad said he was an eff word philanthropist anyway. I'll eat his pancakes from now on, ok? He only ate egg whites, which is gross."

Kelly hugged Sam close and cracked up. "Thanks Sammy. Now get off me and I'll make you my world famous pancakes." Sam trotted out of the room happy he'd solved Kelly's problems.

Kelly rummaged through the cabinets until she found some hazelnut coffee Peggy was probably saving for company and dug some bacon out of the freezer. When everything was ready she yelled for Sam to come eat and poured herself a huge mug of fragrant coffee and added copious amounts of cream and sugar. What the hell? No counting carbohydrates for a while thanks to the philanthropist. Kelly was pretty sure Tim had said philanderer, not philanthropist, but since Sam was going to tell all his friends and they were going to tell their parents she could live with philanthropist. Sam came flying into the room, saw the bacon and chocolate chip pancakes and started to cheer.

"You rock, Aunt Kelly."

Kelly took a bow. "Bon appétit, Sammy. Football is in one hour!" At least it was a home game.

Kelly and Peggy joined the other mothers in the stands. Tim was coming straight from the airport and Sam kept searching the field for him. If he keeps that up Nick will have him running laps. Nick spotted it. Nope, I was wrong Kelly thought. Not laps, pushups.

Tim made it to the game by the second quarter so Kelly left at halftime. Sam had a full night of parental attention ahead of him so Kelly decided to use the opportunity to start packing up her things. She called Matt and let him know she was coming and asked him not to be there.

When Kelly walked in the back door of the kitchen she couldn't believe the mess.

Congealed gravy on plates, dirty frying pans and glasses were on every inch of counter space. Obviously gym girl didn't like to do dishes or clean. There was an open container of Oreo cookies and Kelly helped herself to a handful and got to work packing. Three hours and nine huge garbage bags marked for the Salvation Army later, Matt walked in fresh from the gym.

"Hi Kelly. I told Debbie to drive around the block. So that's it then, you're leaving? Just like that? Can we at least talk?"

Kelly stared at Matt incredulously. "What would you like to talk about, Matt? You didn't want to talk to me before you started screwing around"

Matt leaned back on the counter. "It wasn't like that, Kelly. I really like her. She really likes me. We just started to talk while we were working out. I never really felt that close to you. I love you, though. I don't want us to hate each other. I should have told you before you had to see it.

I'll have your money for you by the end of next month. I'll buy you out of the house at fair market price if you'll sign my car over to me. I want us to be friends."

Kelly snorted and rolled her eyes before she could stop herself.

"You can't tell me you're heartbroken, Kelly. You couldn't wait for me to leave the house every day."

Kelly grabbed a box and headed out to the car. "That's bullshit, Matt. You couldn't wait to leave every day." Even as Kelly was saying it she knew Matt wasn't wrong. She was psyched when he left for work or the gym.

Matt followed Kelly out carrying the biggest box and dragging Max's cage. He loaded them into the back seat and turned to Kelly.

"Ok. I couldn't wait to leave and you were happy I did, so why the anger Kelly?"

Kelly stared at Matt and hissed through her teeth, "Because you lied to me Matt. You lied to me, wasted my time and made me look like an asshole over and over again. That little gym skank felt bad for me. Lot's of different girls felt bad for me. I'm through forgiving and I need you to back off and stop trying to make me understand. If I want to forgive, it'll be when I'm ready, not when you want me to."

Matt searched Kelly's face and gave her a rueful smile. "You're right, Kelly. Take care of yourself. I'll bring the rest of the boxes to Peggy's. For what it's worth, I really am sorry and I love you."

Chapter 5

*K*elly went home and took a long hot shower. She blew out her hair and spent a long time getting her makeup just right. She put on expensive jeans that were supposed to magically lift her butt and pulled her favorite fuchsia cashmere sweater over her head. She stared at herself in the bathroom mirror and added crystal earrings and a matching necklace.

She'd agreed to meet Angie at Bourbon Street Bar and Grill in Nyack. Angie might not like to drink, but she can damn well watch me thought Kelly.

Angie was fresh out of a three month relationship. She'd dumped her latest victim because he didn't like Clint Eastwood. The previous boyfriend got dumped for brushing his teeth before flossing.

"Everyone knows you're supposed to floss first," she'd fumed. "He brought this on himself." She just liked to be single.

Kelly walked in and spotted Angie's platinum head at the bar. As she got closer she realized Angie had company. Nick. Shit. Angie spotted her and started waving her arms in the air.

"Over here Kelly!" Look who I found hunched over a beer by himself"

Kelly rolled her eyes. "Hey Nick. So, what's the story, date didn't show?"

"My date was a burger and beers at the bar, but now that you two are here the night is looking up. Hey Brian," Nick bellowed to the other side of the bar, "Three shots of tequila for me and the girls, and pour one for yourself."

Nick turned to face Kelly. "So Kelly, Angie tells me you moved all your stuff out of the house. Are you moving in with Peggy permanently? I have an extra bedroom you're welcome to. Pay the Utilities and cook occasionally and I'll be happy. What do you say?"

Kelly laughed. "I think I'd cramp your style Nick, but thanks for the offer."

Three hours and countless shots later, Kelly is trying to make a case for the all night diner, Angie and Brian are dragging out the portable karaoke machine from behind the bar and Angie is making out with someone named Paul. She's alternating yelling at Paul for wearing corduroy jeans, and kissing him. After two more rounds and bellowing John Cougar Mellancamp songs at the top of her lungs, Kelly fell asleep on the bar.

Kelly wakes up on Peggy's paisley couch. She starts to panic when she realizes she has no idea how she got there. The last thing she remembers is all of them leaving and getting into a taxi. She remembers Paul saying that Al Pacino lived in Snedens Landing, two minutes away. She remembers remarking that it would be funny if they rang his doorbell and when he opened his door they would all punch their fists in the air and chant "Attica, Attica, Attica."

Oh shit. Kelly looks around in a panic. Where the hell did she leave her cell phone? She grabs Peggy's ancient rotary phone and dials Angie's cell number as quickly as she can, feeling like she might have a nervous breakdown as she watches the dial slowly go back to its place before she can dial the next Number. No answer. She calls Nick next. No answer. Kelly slams the phone down in frustration and it rings almost immediately. She picks it up without thinking and barks hello into the receiver. A man with an Indian accent is on the line.

"Hello, is my new friend Miss Kelly at home?"

"Who, may I ask is calling," Kelly asks with mounting panic. Please do not let this guy be calling to ask me out. What the hell happened last night Kelly thinks, holding her stomach.

"I am her new friend Abdul. I have Miss Kelly's cell phone and you are her emergency contact number, Miss Peggy."

Kelly exhaled sharply.

"Hello Abdul. This is Miss, I mean this is Kelly. Would it be ok if I came and picked up the phone?"

"No problem Miss Peggy. I am at work at the taxi company all day."

"Great Abdul, I'll see you in fifteen minutes. Thanks again."

Kelly grabbed her shoes and car keys and raced out the front door. No car. Damn, Damn, Damn!

She ran back into the house and upstairs to where there was a real phone, not a rotary and hits re-dial. The dispatcher answered and Kelly asked for Abdul and arranged for him to pick her up and drive her to Nyack to pick up her car.

On the way to Nyack Abdul confirmed her worst case scenario. Yes, they had gone to Mr. Pacino's house and chanted Attica, and Mr. Pacino was very gracious about it. He even chuckled, at first. That is, until Kelly started yelling, "I'm out of line, no you're out of line! We're all out of line!" That's when Mr. Pacino took his cell phone out of his bathrobe and called the police. Nick dragged Kelly and Angie back to the cab while Paul tried to persuade "Alby" to come along to the diner with his new friends. At that point Mr. Pacino threw his cell phone at the cab.

"So you see Miss Kelly? There was really no property damage seeing as how Mr. Pacino broke his own phone against my cab. If your friend had not leaned out of the cab to throw up there would have been no mess at all left at Mr. Pacino's house. The police only gave you and your friend's tickets for trespassing and drunken disorderly conduct. Since I was driving, I only got trespassing. You then passed out in my cab and Mr. Nick and I carried you into Miss Peggy's house.

"Your sister Peggy was very nice about the whole episode. I told her what that humorless Mr. Pacino did and she was really quite appalled."

Great, Kelly thought. Peggy knows. Jay might as well have put it in the gossip column. Which unbeknownst to Kelly, he did. He thinly veiled the names of course, but hell, it was Rockland. Even Kelly's Mom knew. Jay's blog read as follows;

"What costume queen and her motley assortment of friends converged on an unsuspecting celebrity in the wee hours of the morning? My sources say they caused quite a stir and left quite a mess! Forget about chanting Attica, they almost ended up there. Fortunately, the celebrity can handle the truth, drunken miscreants who are out of order and he also wields quite a cell phone I'm told. Oh, if only I had been invited on their night of mayhem, this could all have been avoided!"

$\mathcal{W}$ hat the hell was I thinking, Angie fumed. As if the evening hadn't been bad enough. Throwing up on Al Pacino's driveway was a personal best. Angie threw herself down on her chaise lounge. Why couldn't I have just hooked up with corduroy boy? Why did I have to return home and drunk dial, Angie thought woefully.

"Breakfast is ready madam. Come and get it," Jay bellowed from the kitchen.

Angie rolled her eyes and stuck her head under a cushion. Oh my God, it cooks too.

"I have no food Jay. What could you possibly have cooked, freak."

Jay walked into the room, dish towel draped over his shoulder.

"I brought breakfast with me, Angie. It's not like I just met you. By the way, I took some of your makeup and Pepsi out of the fridge to make room for food. Come and eat now stick figure."

Angie got up and stomped to the kitchen table. She stared in disbelief at the array of food. There were fresh berries, crepes, and scrambled eggs with dill and crumbled sausage. If she wasn't mistaken there was also fresh squeezed blood orange juice. There was a loud popping noise and Angie jumped and spun around. Jay was pouring champagne into two fluted glasses. He handed one to Angie who took it while staring at Jay with her mouth hanging open. She downed the contents and when Jay went to refill her glass, grabbed the bottle and started swigging from that.

"Sit down and eat Angie before your bath water gets cold."

Angie bounced her head on the table repeatedly. "Jay, you have to be screwing with me. Who does this shit, who?" Jay sat back in his chair and stared at Angie.

"Eat your breakfast, you ungrateful bitch. I made everything you like and I'm tired of listening to your bullshit." Angie slapped the table.

"Jay, look at me! This is ridiculous."

Jay sighed, reached forward and grabbed the champagne bottle and refilled his glass.

"Ok, Angie, save your breath. I don't want to hear any more of your psychotic crap." He pulled Angie's chair closer, leaned forward and kissed her. Angie felt herself responding. Jay broke the kiss and held Angie's face. "We're going to have a long talk, but first eat your breakfast and take your damn bath so you'll have energy to fight with me. I'm not leaving without an answer this time. If I leave it'll be for good. I need to know that you are at least considering us."

Angie pulled away and glared at Jay. Then she pulled her chair closer to the table and started to eat with the attitude of a person going to the chair. Jay turned to the sink to hide his smile and recalled the day he realized he loved her.

It was at Kelly's wedding reception that he realized he had a problem. He was sitting at the bridesmaids table throwing back gin and tonics. He pulled apart his hand tied silk bow tie and sighed. Kelly looked so beautiful, like

Grace Kelly. Why the hell was she marrying Matt, the nice guy poser? He was so phony. He wasn't even her type. Kelly had always been attracted to the dark swarthy type, just like he was, unfortunately. Nick was much more typical of the kind of guy Kelly usually found appealing. Poor Nick, pining for Kelly, drowning his sorrows at the bar. And there was Angie, dancing with the biggest loser she could find. She'd out done herself this time. The guy wasn't bad looking, but he might as well have had big, dumb asshole written on his back. He had to admit though, Angie looked gorgeous. Red was certainly her color and she looked so elegant, as only a naturally thin person can in a bridesmaids dress. He was surprised Peggy had managed to make Angie wear it. Something about her feet looked odd though. As she moved to the music the dress moved exposing her feet. Jay laughed out loud. Now that makes sense. Angie had worn black army boots under her floor length gown. All was right in the universe again. Her dance partner had to be double her weight and over a foot taller than her. The poor guy had no idea what he was getting himself into.

Jay called out to Angie, "Hey Angie, go easy on him. He's only human."

He raised his glass in mock salute and the guy waved back looking confused. Oh you have no idea buddy, Jay thought laughing. She is so out of your league.

Two hours later Angie sat alone at the bar drinking what looked to be soda, but what Jay suspected from the fumes was a long Island Iced Tea.

"What happened to the linebacker Angie? Are you over him already?" Angie had glared at Jay.

"Maybe I was under him already. Mind your damn business pretty boy. I'm going for a walk. You can come if you want."

Jay had shrugged and followed Angie out of the tent. The moon was full and it illuminated the streets giving everything an ethereal quality. Jay glanced at Angie. She looked so young and sad. Jay reached out and grabbed her hand. Angie looked startled but didn't pull away. They passed a park bench and sat down.

"Did she do the right thing, Jay? Does she see something in Matt that we're just missing?"

Jay exhaled loudly and turned to Angie.

"I've been thinking this through a lot, Angie, and I've come to the only reasonable conclusion I can think of. He must be hung like a donkey."

Angie looked so shocked that Jay started to laugh and Angie joined in. They were both doubled over, Angie leaning into Jay. He put his arm around her. She tilted her head to look up at Jay and he kissed her. They kissed for a long time.

When it was time to leave the wedding, Angie collected her belongings, got in Jay's car and spent the night with him. It was the happiest night of Jay's life. He had been sure Angie felt the same way, but the next day she had ranted about being drunk, not being ready for any complicated relationship, called a cab from her cell phone in the bathroom and stayed there until it arrived. She ran out the front door and jumped in the cab before Jay could try and reason with her. Since that night, they'd hooked up a few times, but Angie always behaved the same way. Well, no more. It was either on or off. Jay was tired of hiding and tired of lying about the way he felt.

Angie came out of the bathroom dressed and ready to fight. Jay had hid her car keys, so there would be no fast exit today.

"Can we not do this Jay? I'm really not in the mood."
Jay walked across the room, put his arms around Angie and
kissed her.

"I'll leave in a minute, Angie. I just need you to know
something. I love you." Angie tried to walk away but Jay
held her tightly.

"I don't care what you say right now. I know you love
me too. But this is it. I'm giving you one week to decide.
If I don't hear from you by then, it's over. No more late
night phone calls, calling me when you dump some loser
you shouldn't have been with in the first place. I've had it.
You're either with me or I'm through with you." Jay
walked to the front door.

"I realize you haven't had an easy life Angie, but pushing me away isn't going to make it any easier." Jay left,
shutting the door behind him self with a loud click.

Chapter 7

*G*rowing up Angie heard the words "not normal behavior" referred to her on a frequent basis. Indignant, she would think "not normal? I never drank the laundry detergent. I never lit hundreds of candles and left them by open windows to keep the devil out. No, I was the one blowing out the candles and calling ambulances when mom was in a manic state." Normal was such an alien concept to Angie. What was normal? What would it feel like to be in a normal family, where her only worries would be getting her homework done and the occasional household chores? Pretty damn good, Angie wagered.

What her school perceived as normal and what she actually lived with on a daily basis were worlds apart. Angie didn't know for sure that her family was any different until middle school. In elementary school the parents were kind and her fellow classmates were naive enough not to really notice anything was out of the norm.

By the time they started middle school, the parents were less gracious and her peers were less kind, if not down right mean. By that time they'd figured out something was seriously wrong with Angie's mother. Her behavior was not normal. Her father was known to drink. Her brother Eddy rode the short bus. Any one of these circumstances would probably have invited ridicule, but all together Angie didn't stand a chance.

Her two older brothers Rob and Charlie seemed chronically depressed. They did what they could to help. They had after school jobs to help with grocery and utility bills and they did the yard work. When Angie was in seventh grade she unofficially became the head of the household for all intents and purposes. She was in charge of cooking, laundry, house cleaning, and the shopping. Emotionally her brothers weren't as strong as she was so they left the care of Eddy, who was autistic, and their mother to Angie.

Her father was in the Merchant Marines so he was rarely home and when he was he wasn't much help. He made sure the mortgage was paid and sent what extra cash he could spare to Angie for groceries. Buddy Longing was the only reason Angie and her siblings weren't put in foster care. Angie tried to be grateful but she just couldn't find it in her heart. Her mother couldn't help being manic depressive, but her father could put the bottle down, damnit. He just didn't want to. Her brothers felt bad for him.

Charlie would sigh, "Do you blame him for drinking Angie? My God, he's had to deal with Mom for his whole life." Their sympathetic attitude towards Buddy Longing infuriated her.

"So have I", Angie would answer acerbically. "The only difference is that I'm not a raging drunk. Besides, I'm the one who deals with her, not you losers!"

When Bella Longing was taking her lithium, she was charming and gracious. She had been a beautiful woman once upon a time. She'd attracted attention effortlessly. She was tall, slim and blond with an ethereal quality that was intriguing. Men would open doors for her and insist on helping her with her grocery bags.

But Bella's illness had taken a toll on her looks as well as her family. She started to look older then her years, and inevitably the day would always come when she'd be convinced she was cured and no longer needed the lithium and everything would fall apart at the seams. She wouldn't sleep for weeks. She stopped showering because the water was poisoned. She would light hundreds of candles and leave them by open windows to keep the evil spirits away. Angie would be up all night blowing candles out, terrified her mother was going to burn the house down and they'd all perish in the fire, or worse in her young mind, end up in foster care.

Bella would call the police with elaborate tales of conspiracy. She'd make huge donations to local causes and when the checks bounced Angie would have to field the irate phone calls. On one memorable occasion Bella painted all the rooms in the house red because she felt it would ward off evil spirits who were trying to steal the souls of her children. Bella would show up at Angie's school wearing her nightgown and demand to see her. She would hug Angie and cry inconsolably.

"Oh Angie, I was so afraid they got to you!" Bella Longing would cry and refuse to leave.

Her classmates would point and laugh. Angie would turn beet red and wish she could disappear. She would pretend she didn't see her supposed friends laughing. As Angie got older she stopped turning red and would get angry. When her classmates would snicker she would turn and glare at them. Her angry "What the fuck are you looking at" soon discouraged any comments. But everyone knew she came from an abnormal family. Angie tried to stay a step ahead of her mother, to minimize the damage, but it took a huge toll. Her mother would get committed over and over again to Rockland State Mental Hospital.

Sometimes Angie would be forced to call the police herself and have her committed, but it was always as a last resort. It killed her to have her mother dragged away. Her biggest fear was that social services would step in and make her and her brothers leave their home, so as much as it broke her heart to make the call, she did it before social services came knocking.

The pressure was enormous and there were times when Angie could feel herself cracking under the effort of appearing normal. At school she would periodically lose her mind.

In sixth grade when Mr. Tellevy reprimanded her in front of the class for failing to hand in a project, Angie got angry and knocked her desk over. She was dragged to the principal's office and given detention for the week. Her teachers had no way of knowing that Angie hadn't slept in days because her mother was lighting candles again.

When Angie punched Marcus in the face at lunch time, no one told her teachers it was because he was laughing that her mother had walked around the neighborhood for the entire weekend in her nightgown and rain boots and that he was calling her brother "special Ed" again. Certainly, Marcus wouldn't tell on himself and Angie would rather be thrown out of school than say anything. Fortunately for Angie, learning came easily and her grades were always in the top ten percent of her class.

Under normal circumstances Angie would have had her pick of schools when she graduated high school. But if she went away, who would take care of Eddy? Eddy was pretty self sufficient at this stage, but he was only fifteen. If she went away he would have to be placed in a group home and Angie couldn't stomach the thought of Eddy in such an impersonal setting. He was the kindest person she'd ever known. He'd get lost in the shuffle. He had a routine at home and took a lot of joy in helping Angie with basic chores. Her brothers wouldn't have the patience to work with him. Her mother was in the mental hospital more than she was out at this stage in her life, so she wasn't as worried about who would care for her. No, Angie decided, Rockland Community College was going to have to suffice.

On her eighteenth birthday Angie was at work at Carmines Beauty Supply Store working the register and answering phones. Her friend Cathy had stopped by with lunch and a birthday cake. The owner and a couple of her co workers all joined in to sing happy birthday and went about their business.

The phone rang and her boss grabbed the nearest extension.

"Hey Angie, phone call for you." They weren't supposed to get personal calls but Carmine knew her family situation and didn't bust her chops. She was a good worker and Carmine had been in business long enough to know he was lucky to have her.

Angie grabbed the phone. It was Mr. Pook, the owner of a small deli down the street from her house. He wasn't known for his charm. "Hey Angie, your mother was in here this morning and she stole my eyeglasses off the counter and took off. I need them back today. I can't read the damn prices on anything. I think it's time to call the nut house and have her picked up again. If you don't do it I will." He hung up abruptly.

Angie put her head down on the counter. He was such a jerk, but Angie couldn't blame him for being mad. Bella did seem to bust his chops when she was sick.

While Angie had been on the phone, Cathy noticed something odd going on in the shop window across the street.

"Angie, take a look at the candy store window."

Angie looked up and saw a woman wearing a nightgown and horn rimmed glasses with her face and hands pressed up against the glass.

"Oh shit," Angie exclaimed. "Cathy, do me a favor and just answer the phones for a couple of minutes, ok? That's my Mom!"

Angie ran across the street and entered the crowded candy store. "Mom, what are you doing here," she hissed between her teeth.

Bella looked around to make sure no one was listening. "Look at this," she said dramatically. She stuck the newspaper crossword puzzle under Angie nose. All the little boxes were filled with the number six.

Angie sighed heavily. "Mom, you wrote the sixes in." She grabbed the paper impatiently from Bella. "You need to get back on your lithium before they take you away again."

Bella ripped the paper out of Angie's hands. "Why doesn't anyone believe me? I need to get to the police and show them."

Angie tried to grab her mother but Bella dodged her and ran for the back exit. Unfortunately, she missed the first step and rolled down the other fifteen. An ambulance was called and Bella was brought to the hospital where she received medical treatment for a broken leg and then was committed to Rockland State Mental Hospital involuntarily.

Within two days she was making phone calls to everyone she knew with conspiracy theories. She called Angie to complain that the "psycho killer", aka her husband had come to visit and had brought her chocolates that were too sweet when what she wanted was cigarettes.

Angie talked to her for ten minutes and was finally able to get off the phone when Bella became convinced someone was listening to their conversation.

Two weeks after her mother was committed yet again, Angie came home to find her two brothers and her father at the kitchen table. She hadn't seen or heard from her father in ten months, although he'd continued to pay the mortgage and send home cash. He motioned Angie to come sit at the table. She did as she was asked and refused to look at him.

Buddy Longing sighed. "Angie, I retired three months ago. I have a nice pension. I got a security job thirty hours a week at the mall. But more importantly, I've been sober for one year now." Angie stared at her father in shock. "I didn't say anything before now because I was afraid I would fall off the wagon, but not anymore. I still go to meetings everyday, but it's getting so I look forward to getting up in the mornings. I've been talking to your brothers for months now and we're all in agreement. You need to go away to school and get the education you earned." Angie started to shake her head angrily, but Buddy put his hand up and asked her to please let him finish.

"You earned a full scholarship. We'll look after Eddy and Bella. It's your turn to have a life. You can come home periodically to check up on us, but this is non negotiable. I can't make the past up to you, but I want to help you have a future. Please Angie, it's what Bella would want if she was herself right now."

Eddy clapped his hands. "Angie, I'll do the housework. I'll do the housework!"

Angie looked up at Eddy's happy face. "I know you will Eddy. You always do a great job."

Angie panicked after Jay's ultimatum and true to form had called him six days and twenty three hours later and asked if he was alright with taking it slow.

Jay had calmly replied that even though she'd taken her sweet ass time calling him back, he was willing to take it slow within reason. There had to be some ground rules. They needed to see each other at least three times a week, no exceptions.

Angie had angrily hung up the phone. Jay waited patiently and half an hour later Angie had called back, yelled, "fine, have it your way, control freak" into the phone and hung up.

Chapter 8

*K*elly made a quick call to Sherry asking her to open up the costume store and work the morning shift. With that taken care of, Kelly drove home, let herself into the house, ran for the bathroom and threw up.

Kelly woke up to the sound of the phone ringing three hours later. She opened her eyes tentatively and when it didn't kill her, she attempted to sit up. Yeah, I'll live she decided, but not without a little regret. She looked around and tried to figure out where she'd left her phone. She remembered putting it down on the kitchen counter. She ran and answered on the fourth ring.

"Hi Kelly, how are you feeling this morning," Peggy asked, her voice dripping sarcasm. Pacino called for you. He's remaking "Saturday Night Fever" and wants to know if you're available."

"Very Funny Peg, what's up?" Peggy stopped laughing.

"Sam has football at four forty five. His equipment is in the hallway. Tell Nick he's a great example. He should make himself run laps."

Kelly pulled into the parking lot and Sam ran out of the car like a shot, terrified that he'd have to run laps. Kelly gathered up her huge iced coffee and folding chair and made her way to the other parents. They were all trying not to laugh.

Kelly stopped abruptly. Dan Sullivan was the middle of the group. Dan worked the night shift with the New City Police Department. He spotted Kelly and yelled up to her, "Hey Kelly, no, you're out of Line!"

With that, all the parents lost it. Judy laughed so hard she fell off her chair. From her position on the ground she pumped her fist in the air and chanted, "Attica, Attica!"

"Oh my God Kelly, you need to get out more, girl!"

It's going to be a long, long, season Kelly thought with a sigh.

Nick ran over with a grin.

"It's all taken care of Kelly. Matt's not happy about it, but that's just too bad. He said he'd drop the rest of your stuff to my place tonight. He said as long as I helped him move it you could take the treadmill so we'll take care of that tomorrow."

Judy got up off the ground and walked over to stare at Kelly. "What's going on here? Are you two shacking up?"

Kelly shook her head angrily. "Absolutely not. Nick, what are you talking about?"

Nick laughed.

"You said you thought it was a great idea last night, Kelly."

Kelly glares at Nick incredulously.

"Really Nick? Did Al Pacino think it was a great idea too?"

"Why would we discuss it with him?" Nick replied with a straight face. "I doubt he'll care where you live after Angie puking and what not, but we could have Abdul drive us over and see what he thinks if that'll make you happy."

Kelly glared at Nick until he finally started to laugh.

"Last night I suggested you rent my spare bedroom and you agreed it was a good idea, this was before Abdul and Pacino. Come on Kelly, I could use the extra income and you'll never even see me. I'm at football every night and work all day."

Kelly started to laugh. "Yeah Nick, you're a great influence."

Nick laughed again.

"Everything was fine, Kelly, until you told Pacino "you can't handle the truth!" That's when he got pissed off." Doing his best Al Pacino impersonation, Nick mimicked "That's Jack Nicholson dumbass, get the hell off my property."

Everyone had been doing a great job pretending not to listen to their conversation up until this point, but with that last comment all the parents lost it again, and Judy actually lost bladder control and yelled out for Kelly to please drop her son Gilby off at the end of the practice, as she waddled off in her wet jeans.

Angie pulled into a parking stop at The Spectum School and locked up her car. Cars had been getting robbed in the lot lately and her gym bag was there. Her sneakers were worth more to her than her car. Angie was a special education teacher who worked with the mentally handicapped. She was in a vile mood and spoiling for a fight. Her head teaching assistant Mark took one look at her face, handed her a huge caramel Latte and gave her a hug.

"Ok, before you make one of the new Teaching Assistants cry, just tell me what happened before anyone gets here. We have twenty minutes, so start talking."

Angie gave him a rough outline, even adding in the Al Pacino incident. By the time she had relayed the bulk of the story, Mark was hysterical.

"Oh my God, you met Al Pacino!"

Kelly gave Mark her most withering glare. "You are missing the point, dumbass. What do I do about Jay?"

Mark laughed. "I think you should stop thinking about it so much and just try spending some time with him, Angie. Why do you have to worry about something that might just be a bit of fun? Hang out with him. Just give him a chance. He dresses so nice, it'll be hard for you to pick him apart and dump him, that's for sure."

There was a knock on the door. Angie looked up as a delivery man walked in carrying a huge bouquet of weird looking flowers. Oh, it was a fruit bouquet. Jay probably figured, and rightly so, that she would have tossed flowers, but the fruit she'd feel compelled to share with the kids.

Mark shook his head. "I don't know Angie. This one may be really hard to pick apart."

Angie spent the rest of the day terrifying the Teachers' Aids, with the exception of Mark. She just wanted them to do their jobs. Was that asking too much? Was it asking the impossible? Two of them apparently didn't own watches and would stroll in twenty minutes late at least three times a week and one, Nakia, called in sick at least once a week. When she was there she was very hard working and kind to the kids. She was also a huge pain in the ass.

"You need to get laid, Angie," Nakia would tell her every day. "Stop being so picky and find yourself a man, girl. You ain't getting any younger and you're only getting meaner, which I thought was impossible."

Angie glared at Nakia, which only made her laugh.

"See? You're just proving me right! You could peel paint off the wall with that face, bitch."

Angie ignored her and called the children to join her in morning group. They pulled their chairs to the front of the room in a semi- circle and started to sing about the days of the week and the weather.

Most of the kids in the room were very low functioning. It could be very disheartening. Every once in a while you really felt like you got through to one of the children, like teaching Martin to say five different words when he'd never spoken before at fifteen years old.

And some days were just out right funny. Like the day a new teaching assistant had come into the room for the first time, having never worked with the mentally handicapped before wearing perfume that smelled like cotton candy. The look on her face as she was surrounded by eight large teenagers was priceless. They couldn't figure out where she'd hid it and were busy looking.

Morning group was just winding down when a different delivery man appeared at the door with a huge bouquet of star gazer lilies and a gift wrapped box. He looked around the room.

"Is there an Angie here?" he said hopefully.

Nakia let out a whoop and grabbed the card.

"Who the hell is Jay? Wait, isn't he your gorgeous gay friend? Tell me you did not get yourself a beard so you don't have to date. You are beyond hopeless bitch. I need coffee."

Mark was beside himself. "Open the box already, Kelly. You're killing me." Nakia smiled, "Oh, if only that were true Mark."

Kelly tore off the paper and inside there were an expensive pair of running shoes. Angie read the card. "You can run, but you can't hide, not anymore. With love and definitiveness, Jay."

Angie snorted. We'll see about that, buddy.

Chapter 9

*K*elly finished unpacking the rest of her clothes and dropped onto the bed exhausted. The Sleepy's delivery men had set the bed up and left over an hour ago. She was very glad she spent the extra money for the upgraded mattress. Kelly took the time to admire her paint job while she was laying flat on her back. She'd picked wedge wood blue for the walls and a thick down comforter in the matching blue with tiny white and lilac flowers. Her antique mirror and dresser balanced out one wall and there was a decent sized walk in closet with a shoe rack.

"The room looks terrific Kelly," Nick said from the doorway. "Do you want to grab some dinner to celebrate, my treat?"

Kelly looked at Nick, silhouetted in the doorway. He really was very handsome, Kelly mused, with those long black lashes framing grey eyes and his full head of black hair.

"I'd love to Nick, but my Uncle Mike and Aunt Danis are at my mom's and I promised her I wouldn't leave her alone with them. I have to be there in forty five minutes. "Why don't you come with me? It's usually a fun evening," Kelly said with a straight face.

An hour and ten minutes later, Nick found out just how much fun.

"Kelly, get the bottle of Jamison's and bring it here, sure and make yourself useful," Uncle Mike bellowed. "Nick my young fiend, I mean friend, let's drink to your health. Where are my fags?"

"Excuse me sir?" Nick asked looking completely floored.

"My cigarettes lad, what did you think I meant gob-shite?" Uncle Mike felt his shirt pockets, followed by his pants pockets. "Danis, the baby's got my fags again, bloody hell!"

Kelly ran to the back door and looked out. Sure enough, there was her eight year old cousin Maureen smoking while she sat on the swing.

Uncle Mike looked out the door. "Oh sure now, she's just being precocious. Pay her no mind and she'll stop."

Kelly ran across the backyard and yanked the cigarette from Maureen's mouth, threw it on the ground and stepped on it angrily.

"Bad girl Maureen, don't ever do that again!"

Uncle Mike looked affronted. "Come now Kelly, don't get your knickers in a twist. Maureen is just trying to get our attention. Now you've shown her how to get it. Poorly done Kelly," he said with a shake of his head.

"Uncle Mike, if she colors on a wall, no problem. But you can't let her smoke!" Kelly heard a snort and turned to see Nick shoot whiskey out his nose. When Kelly glared at him he made a gallant effort to keep a straight face, but had to leave the room quickly when he realized he was losing the battle.

"Now Nick, don't be shooting good whiskey out your nose. For one thing, it's a mortal sin. For another, Mo is looking right at you and we don't want her to get ideas. If she starts to shoot whiskey out her nose Kelly will be all over you like a cheap suit," Uncle Mike bellowed.

Uncle Mike's parenting skills were infamous among the Moriarty clan. Kelly's father Patrick swore it was because he'd hit his head one too many times. Whatever the reason was, her father's baby brother was a piece of work as her mother Poppy liked to say.

When Sam was little Uncle Mike and Aunt Danis had taken him to the beach for a long weekend. When they arrived home, Sam had gotten out of the car with his hand over his nose and had run into the house. Apparently he'd kept climbing a fence at the beach and Uncle Mike had gotten tired of pulling him off it so he'd made up the story of "Naughty No Nose" the boy who'd lost his nose because he wouldn't listen to his parents and stop climbing things. Uncle Mike had gone into great detail about the accident that had befallen Naughty and how people screamed when they saw him. Sam had listened with horror etched all over his face. It had worked. Sam climbed no more fences on that vacation. He also wet the bed and slept with a light on for a month.

hree long hours later, Kelly put her feet on Nick's coffee table and took a large gulp of her martini.

Nick sat down next to Kelly, laughing. "Well, that was entertaining. Are they available for children's parties and Bar Mitzvahs?"

Kelly snorted. "If you think that's bad, you should see Uncle Mike in his Robin Hood costume at Halloween, green tights and all," Kelly said shuddering. "No amount of candy is worth that."

Nick laughed and plopped himself down on the couch, just a little too close for comfort, Kelly thought to herself.

"I had a great time, Kelly. Thanks for letting me come with you. Do you have any interest in watching a movie?"

Kelly shook her head. "No thanks, Nick. I have an early start tomorrow. I'm going to call it a night."

Safely ensconced in her room, Kelly climbs under her new comforter and feeling strangely unsettled, thinks back to college.

It had been the night of the first football game of the season. They'd lost and Matt was in an unusually bad mood. He picked a fight with Kelly and stormed off. Kelly was embarrassed and trying not to cry. Nick sat down next to her, popped the top on a beer and handed it to her. Kelly mumbled a thank you and took a long pull from the icy can. She felt a warm hand on her face. Nick gently wiped her tears with his thumb.

"Don't get upset, Kelly. You know it's not about you. He's just a shitty loser, has been since birth. When he lost his first tooth, he got into a fist fight with the tooth fairy."

Kelly, who was in mid swig, spit Budweiser on her new Sketchers. Laughing, she turned to look at Nick who was now so close their noses were an inch apart. He smoothed Kelly's hair back off her face and stared at her just a little too long. Then with the air of someone who just woke up, he shook his head to clear it and jumped to his feet.

"Another beer, Kelly or are you calling it a night?"

Kelly shook her head, wondering why she felt a let down at Nicks departure from her side. "No thanks, Nick. I think I'll call it a night. I'm wiped."

Nick reached down and pulled Kelly to her feet. "Me too," Nick said. "I'll walk you back."

The moon was huge and bright with a slightly orange tint. A true "harvest moon." It was Kelly's favorite time of the year. The air was crisp and fresh with the scent of apples from the local orchard and tangy with the smoky scent from the bonfire.

Nicks fingers brushed Kelly's and she felt an electric jolt and pulled her hand away.

They reached the dorm and Nick held the door open. The first floor was unusually quiet. Everyone was still at the bonfire. Nick pushed the button on the elevator. They rode together to the third floor in silence. Kelly was feeling the effects of one too many bonfire beers and trying hard to make sense of what she was feeling.

"How about we put a movie on, Kelly? I've got a six pack and some chips in my room. Come on, you don't feel like being alone, right? I'll go get the supplies, you pick out a movie and I'll meet you back in your room."

Nick took off before Kelly could argue. She walked into her unlocked room and was bowled over by the heavy scent of musk.

Angie had left black scented candles burning on every flat surface.

Kelly started the process of blowing them out while she waited for Nick. Her antique chest had melted wax all over the top. Kelly cursed and grabbed the candle, spilling hot wax down the length of her Henley tee-shirt. She pulled the shirt over her head and threw it into her hamper, pulling off her jeans as well. She rummaged through what was left of her clean cloths and pulled out pink flannel pajama bottoms. She quickly pulled them on and was in the process of pulling on a tank top when the bedroom door flew open smacking Kelly right in the head, knocking her flat on her back. Kelly threw the tank top at him angrily.

"Damn it, Nick, what the hell!"

Nick kicked the door shut.

"Oh my God, Kelly, are you ok? Holy shit, I'm so sorry."

Kelly started to laugh and cry from the pain at the same time.

"Damn, Nick, that hurt like hell!"

Nick picked Kelly up off the floor and placed her on the bed, lying down next to her. He felt her head to see how large the bump was and started to laugh with her. "I thought the hangover was gonna do you in tomorrow, but it's got competition now." They laughed together for a few more minutes and then the room seemed to get very quiet. They lay next to each other in companionable silence looking at each other, listening to the sound of their breathing. Nick inched forward and pulled Kelly close so that their bodies meshed together from head to toe. He kissed Kelly's face, starting at her forehead, then each temple, her eyelids, her nose and finally her lips. Kelly was completely lost in the moment.

When the door flew open slamming into the dresser, Kelly and Nick jumped apart. Angie stared at them in a drunken haze and walked back out, leaving the door open in her wake.

Kelly hurriedly pulled the tank over her head and ran to the TV and put a movie on. They heard yelling in the hallway and Angie reappeared wearing a football helmet. She walked into the closet and shut the door behind herself.

Two minutes later a big, burly, red head named Jud stuck his head in the doorway.

"Did either of you see that crazy little blond? She just took off with my football helmet!"

Kelly put her head under her pillow.

"Nope, but if we see her wearing a helmet, I'll make sure to get it back for you Jud," Nick replied with a straight face.

"Thanks Nick. See you tomorrow." Jud left closing the door behind him.

Nick stayed on the bed and pretended to watch the movie. Kelly sprawled on Angie's bed and tried to pay attention, but the tension in the room was too distracting and Kelly was more aware of Nick then she was of the movie's story line. At some point during the movie Angie crawled out of the closet and curled up at the end of her bed next to Kelly's feet, still wearing Jud's helmet. As the credits were rolling Matt walked through the door and smiled.

"I had a feeling Angie had Jud's helmet. He'll be happy to see it again. Hey Nick, thanks for walking my girl home."

Nick stared at Matt. "Not a problem, Mat." He turned and looked at Kelly, who was pretending to be asleep. He stood up and stretched as Matt walked over and picked Kelly up off of Angie's bed and deposited her on her own bed, pulling her comforter up over her body. He turned to Nick. "Come on, let's go grab a beer."

Nick shook his head. "I'm going to call it a night, Matt. We have a long day tomorrow." Matt shrugged. "Suit your self," and proceeded to lie down next to Kelly. Nick stared at Matt. "On second thought Matt, let's grab that beer." Matt jumped up and high fived Nick. "Now you're talking. Let's go."

Kelly's phone rang an hour later. She picked up the receiver. "You felt it too, Kelly." Kelly couldn't think of anything to say. She did feel it, but she was with Matt, and she loved him, didn't she?

"Goodnight, Nick" she replied, returning the phone to its cradle. She was awake a long time staring at the ceiling that night.

Kelly was running on her treadmill at 7:00 am while Max barked at her from the sidelines.

"I'll take you out for a walk when I'm done. Please shut up!"

Nick had left to go running an hour ago and probably would have taken Max with him if he wasn't still mad at him for peeing on his new cross trainer running shoes. The TV was on full blast so she didn't hear her cell phone ring until Max went and got it and spit it out in front of the treadmill. Kelly jumped off and picked it up.

"That's great Max. Thanks for the slobber," Kelly said sarcastically, shaking off the phone. "Hello?"

"It's Uncle Mike love. We're driving to the shore for the weekend and Peggy said you and Sam would love to come with us. We'll be round in forty minutes to pick you up, cheers!"

Her phone rang again, but this time it was Peggy.

"Peggy, I'll kill you! What the hell were you thinking?"

Peggy cut her off.

"Look Kelly, take one for the team, he's driving everyone crazy, and I can't send Sam alone. Uncle Mike might accidently lose him. Plus, Sam really wants to go. I'll pay for everything! Just bring your swimsuit."

Kelly snorted unattractively.

"Oh, you're going to pay alright Peggy, trust me on that one."

"Aunt Eileen found God, Kelly. Apparently he was missing. I'd like to know where she found him, post office wall? Did she see him on a milk carton?"

Uncle Mike turned to look at Kelly.

"Now Michael Patrick, stop it," Aunt Danis laughed.

"Just be glad about it for the love of God. She's much more pleasant to be around now that she's afraid of hell. Kelly, I can't wait until you see the hotel. It's got a huge pool and a gym!"

Sam could barely contain himself in the backseat. "You promised I could swim with the fishes, Uncle Mike!"

Uncle Mike chortled.

"Now Sam, what I said was, keep it up and someday you'll be swimming with the fishes!"

Kelly rolled her eyes. "That's really nice, Uncle Mike."

The hotel wasn't the Taj Mahal like Aunt Danis had imagined, but all in all Kelly was impressed. It was a beautifully maintained older hotel, which did in fact have a pool. They parked the car, checked in and headed up to their rooms. Sam and Kelly had a room adjacent to Uncle Mike, Aunt Danis, and Maureen.

Kelly handed the credit card key to Sam who opened the door excitedly.

"It's got two double beds, Aunt Kelly."

Sam hopped onto the bed closest to the bathroom.

"Mine," Sam yelled gleefully. "I have a bladder the size of a pea!"

Kelly cracked up.

"Just let me brush my hair and put on my swimsuit and I'll be ready to go."

"I'll brush it for you, Aunt Kelly"

Kelly laughed. "No way, Sam. The last time you tried to brush it Matt had to cut the brush out."

Sam leveled Kelly with his best look of contempt. "That was a whole year ago. I'm much more mature now."

Kelly laughed and closed the bathroom door behind her. "And my hair is much shorter now Sam. Thanks just the same."

Six hours later, Kelly had had quite enough of the beach.

"That's it, Sam! Get out of the water now!"

Sam waved and smiled, riding the next big wave with his boogie board. Uncle Mike walked to the edge of the water.

"Sam, get out now for the love of God, we're all famished!"

Sam waved and continued to swim.

"By God, that child loves to swim. He looks like one of them killer whales. What's his name? Shamu! Hey Shamu! Get the hell out of the water," Uncle Mike bellowed at the top of his lungs.

It took forty minutes, but they finally coaxed Sam out of the water. Back at the hotel they showered, dressed and headed out for a nice dinner at Kelly's favorite restaurant at the shore, "The Lobster Shanty."

The dinner was wonderful, especially after Kelly ordered a bottle of decent champagne for the table and handed the waiter Peggy's credit card for the whole check. The only nerve wracking moment was when Sam accidently on purpose shot a grape tomato across the room where it landed in a very large obnoxious looking man's martini. Gin splashed everywhere, covering his shirt and sprinkling his wife who dropped her wine glass on the table, adding to the mess. Sam ducked under the table as the man glared around the restaurant looking for the culprit. When he couldn't figure out where it had come from, he made due with complaining to the waitress who knew damn well where it had come from, but wasn't telling. She glared at Sam intensely and nodded at Uncle Mike. A large tip was understood.

On the way back to the hotel they decided to walk down the boardwalk and buy Sam an ice cream cone. It was a perfect beach night. The sun was setting in tones of pink and orange and there was a slight breeze. Kelly felt relaxed and happy. She looked down at Sam who was being unusually quiet.

"Penny for your thoughts, Sam?"

Sam looked up at his aunt.

"I love you, Aunt Kelly. I just wish my mom was here. She's always saying don't wish your life away, but she doesn't get it. Life goes quickly and she's not here with us. She's not part of it, part of me. It's sad that she doesn't have so many of the memories that we have."

Kelly looked down at Sam's upturned sun kissed face. He looked so sad and so full of wisdom beyond his years. He got it. He understood what was important.

There was poor Peggy trying to make a better life for Sam by working a ton of hours when all he wanted was to have her around. He didn't care about their beautiful house or cars. Frankly, he'd be more comfortable in a house where he wasn't afraid to scuff the walls or break something. Kelly sighed.

"I know Sam. Maybe we'll have an intervention and try and talk to her, ok?"

Sam smiled, hope lighting up his face. "Do you think that'll work, Aunt Kelly?"

Kelly smiled. "I think it can't hurt, right?"

Sam smiled and shrugged in agreement. He let go of Kelly's hand and stared at a house up ahead with a three foot inflatable pool. A mischievous look crossed his face and he broke into a run. Kelly looked from the pool to Sam's running form and yelled, "No Sam, don't!"

There were three older couples sitting around a small glass table about two feet from the pool. Their table was laid out with hors devours and sparkling glasses of wine. Candles sparkled merrily in the twilight. They were smiling and people watching as groups of people passed them on the boardwalk. They saw Sam running and they were still smiling, having no idea what was about to befall them.

A couple of feet from the group Sam veered to the right and cannon balled into the pool, sending a tidal wave over the small table and soaking the three couples. Wine glasses went flying off the table along with the neatly laid out snacks. Kelly looked on in horror. Well, this is one memory Peggy will just have to live without. Apparently the story of "Naughty No Nose" was no longer a deterrent Kelly thought, shaking her head.

Kelly finally got Sam situated and into bed. His teeth were brushed, his prayers were said and Kelly was exhausted. Uncle Mike knocked on the door separating the rooms and walked in.

"Now, young Sam, I hope you had fun today. But remember, God sees everything. He sees you when you're sleeping, he knows when you're awake, he knows when you've been bad or good, so be good for goodness sake."

Sam rolled his eyes at Kelly.

"Um, Uncle Mike? I'm pretty sure that's Santa Claus, not God."

Uncle Mike didn't seem concerned with this news.

"Well young Sam, he's a smart guy too! And he's always watching, always watching."

Uncle Mike raised his eyebrows, stared at Sam and backed out of the room slowly while maintaining eye contact. Sam stared at Kelly.

"Aunt Kelly, can I ask you something?"

Kelly was trying to keep a straight face.

"Sure Sam, what's up?"

Sam pointed to the adjacent room.

"Does Uncle Mike have brain damage?"

Kelly struggled even harder to keep a neutral face.

"No Sam, he's just special," Kelly replied using finger quotes around the word special. Sam cracked up.

"Well, we'll see how special you think he is tomorrow," Sam replied, mimicking Kelly's finger quotes. "He's got a surprise for you." Sam fell asleep still chortling softly to himself.

The next morning Kelly woke up to a gorgeous day. It was autumn crisp with the smell of saltwater. Kelly tied her sneakers and pulled her hair back with an elastic band. She knocked on the adjoining door and let Aunt Danis know she was going for a run. Maureen bounded into the room to lay in bed watching cartoons with Sam.

Kelly ran on the sand until her legs ached and her lungs hurt. She took her sneakers off and let the water cover her feet and ankles. She walked back up to the boardwalk, rinsed the sand off her feet and sat on a bench completely exhausted.

When the desire for coffee overcame her need to relax, she shoved her feet into her shoes and walked to the fragrant bakery across the street from the hotel. Mimi's Bakery was crowded considering how early it was, but the line moved quickly and Kelly got four coffees, two milks and six huge cinnamon rolls, dripping with thick, white icing. She paid her bill, grabbed her packages and started to walk out. She bumped into a familiar broad chest. She looked up and Nick laughed at her expression. "Am I to take it that you didn't need me to come here immediately?"

Kelly rolled her eyes, exasperated. "What the hell is Uncle Mike up to now," she fumed. Nick laughed and took the packages from Kelly.

"Well, whatever it is, it won't be boring."

"Now Kelly, we'd like to spend a little quality time with Sam, so be a good lass and you and Nick go out on the town tonight. We're taking Sam to Seaside to hang out with the floozies and ride some of them unstable looking rides. Great fun, so I'm told. Here's a twenty for your first round. Now go and have fun for God's sake. Get the pole out of your arse."

"I think your Uncle is trying to set us up, Kelly."

Kelly stared at Nick. "Really Nick, what was your first clue?"

"Well. Just so you know Kelly, I'm not going to put out just because you had your Uncle drag me all the way down here. You could have just asked me out yourself."

Kelly turned to stare at Nick who gave her his best demure look from under his eyelashes.

"You better buy me at least two drinks. I'm not a cheap date."

"That's not what they said at college, Nick," Kelly replied with a smirk.

"Well you heard wrong Missy. Not that it matters, but I only came to hang out with Uncle Mike and Sam. I figured I'd have to bail them out of jail by the end of the weekend anyway, so I might as well come hang out. So don't even think about getting fresh with me. Even if you begged me, I'm not giving you any. So forget it."

Kelly rolled her eyes and laughed. "I'll try and contain myself around your deadly charms, Nick."

Nick wagged his eyebrows up and down.

"Good. Now go get dressed in something "Snookie" or better yet "J-Wow" and let's hit the Tiki bar."

Four hours and three shots of tequila plus drinks later, Kelly was feeling no pain. The air was crisp and chilly and the bar wasn't crowded. Most of the summer crowd was gone so it was just the locals and a second rate band, but to Kelly it sounded amazing. Colorful lights surrounded the stage and the dance floor was nearly empty with the exception of Kelly. Nick sat at the table and watched Kelly dance. She looked young, happy and a little on the tipsy side. Her dress swirled around her legs and her light weight cardigan was form fitting. She looked comfortable in her own skin. Nick was happy just to watch her. He thought back to May of their senior year.

It had been a hot, humid night with no breeze. Nick had been at a local hang out called "The Mason Jar" with friends. Matt had stayed in to study. Nick missed the last bus and had to walk the two miles home. He'd given his jacket to a female friend to wear in the chilly bar and he forgot he'd left his front door keys in the pocket so of course the front door, which was usually unlocked, was locked. He gave the door a frustrated kick and waited, but nobody came to let him in. Probably all passed out by now, Nick thought.

Matt's light was out and Nick knew from past experience that he could light the house on fire and Matt wouldn't wake up. He grabbed the gutter and started to pull himself up the side of the house. Matt's window was slightly cracked to let air in and

Nick figured he could push it open and climb in with minimal effort. He finished climbing, hooked his arm over the windowsill and hauled himself in.

There was Matt, lying naked with a red headed sophomore from their sister sorority. Nick thought her name was Tara, but he wasn't positive. They were both staring at Nick with their mouths hanging unattractively open. Nick mumbled an apology and got the hell out of the room as fast as he could. Matt went running after him with a sheet wrapped around his waist.

"Nick, don't tell anyone, please. I can't let Kelly find out, it would kill her." "Are you planning on breaking up with her or what, Matt?"

Matt laughed, "of course not. Tara doesn't matter. She knew I had a girlfriend, she knows the deal. She's seeing somebody also, so it's not a big deal."

Nick glared at Matt. "How could you do this to Kelly, Matt?"

"You're not seriously lecturing me about relationships, right Nick? You're a bit too much of a player to pull off this sanctimonious shit. It's none of your freaking business, it's between me and Kelly. Why do you suddenly give a shit about her feelings, anyway?"

Nick pushed past Matt and headed to his room. "I always gave a shit, Matt. You just didn't pay attention. You need to tell her. Break it off, she's not a toy. You have two days to tell her. If you don't, I will."

Twenty four hours later Matt and Kelly were engaged.

Kelly walked barefoot on the warm sand, the sound of the waves soothing her nerves. Nick walked beside her, his fingertips brushing her hand.

"You always knew it wouldn't work out with me and Matt, didn't you Nick?" Kelly asked looking up at him.

"I didn't think he deserved you, Kelly. Matt's not a bad guy, but he's never going to love someone as much as he loves himself. I just think you deserve better than that. I always wished that I'd made my move on you faster, that I hadn't had a girlfriend."

Nick put his arms around Kelly and Kelly was reaching to put her arms around Nick when her cell phone rang, startling both of them and breaking the mood.

Kelly dropped her shoes in the sand to free her hands. She routed through her pocketbook, grabbed her cell phone and checked the caller ID. It looked like the hotels phone number.

"Hello? He did what? We'll be right there!"

Kelly hung up the phone and stormed up the beach to the wooden steps that led to the boardwalk.

"Uncle Mike gave Sam a Red Bull and went to sleep. He was running laps around the hotel floors when the manager grabbed him and made him call me. Apparently he was banging on peoples doors and yelling "room service" as he ran."

They ran the four blocks back to the hotel where the irate evening manager had Sam behind the check in desk.

"Stop touching things," he bellowed at Sam as Kelly ran up to the desk.

The manager spun around and Kelly read his name tag. John Ivers.

"Mr. Ivers, I am so sorry," Kelly babbled.

Mr. Ivers glared at Kelly and hissed from between clenched teeth, "Just get him out of my sight. What kind of maniac would give this kid a Red Bull?"

Sam chirped, "It's a vitamin drink. It's good for me," and tried to run away.

Nick kept a firm hold on his arm.

"Once again, I'm very sorry," Kelly said dragging Sam towards the elevator before Mr. Ivers could articulate exactly what he thought about Sam's last statement. Kelly yelled over her shoulder, "We'll be checking out tomorrow, I promise!"

Mr. Ivers ran towards Nick and handed him a roll of duct tape. "Just in case you need it," he said and ran back to the front desk. Sam tried to duck around Kelly to go back to Mr. Ivers, who looked alarmed. Kelly got him in an impressive headlock and pushed the elevator button for the third floor with her toe.

Nick was laughing so hard he was doubled over clutching his side.

"Oh man, if I had only filmed that with my phone. Sam, you deserve the academy award for "most annoying child in a hotel."

Kelly glared at Nick.

"Thanks Nick, you've been tremendously helpful. Help me hold Sam down, now!"

Kelly woke up at 6AM on the hotel's full size bed with Sam and Nick.

When Sam had finally passed out after what felt like one hundred rounds of "go fish", they had laid him down between each other to make sure he didn't escape. Kelly also made sure the security chain was engaged in case Sam managed to get out of the bed unnoticed and decided to go wandering. Nick was still out cold. He looked different when he was sleeping, uncomplicated and young. Kelly stared at his face. She thought back to the day of her wedding.

They had decided to save money and have the wedding in the backyard. Matt had wanted a pig roast and eventually he won out. The tent was set up and the caterers were hard at work.

It was a chilly overcast September day and there was a slight mist in the air. Kelly was glad she'd chosen a long sleeved gown. It was a heavy silk in a creamy off white, low cut with beautiful crystals hand sewn over the entire dress. Peggy had picked out a long sleeved dress as well, in a deep wine color with almost no back. Angie had balked about it, but it looked even better on her than it did on Peggy. Kelly was glad it was full length as Angie had worn black Doc Martins with it.

The tent looked enchanted in the moonlight. It was strung with fairy lights and all the tables had hundreds of tea lights, as well as white tapered candles. There were gorgeous arrangements of red roses, as well as rose petals strewn on the tables. The wedding went off without a hitch. The limo pulled onto Kelly's street. The driver swore he could see the tent from two blocks away.

As the guests entered the tent they were handed a glass of champagne with raspberries. After the bride and groom were announced, Kelly and Matt went from table to table to greet their guests and thank them for helping them to celebrate. Kelly couldn't imagine a more relaxed, perfect night. There were disposable cameras on every table so their guests could take pictures for them to enjoy. Nice, candid shots. All in all, it was a beautiful, elegant, easy going affair. Maybe a little too relaxed.

Nick had put cans of silly string on all the tables. Kelly shrugged off her annoyance. With Matt's friends, it could have been a lot worse. Silly string wasn't that bad. The DJ announced the couple's first official dance as husband and wife. Matt and Kelly made their way out to the dance floor. They'd chosen to dance to "You light up my Life", an irony Kelly would laugh about later. As they danced around the small wooden floor, Kelly watched in annoyance as Nick and Bill Camden, a friend from high school, took aim with the silly string.

Unfortunately, as the silly string sailed through the air, it passed through one of the lit candles and ignited. Matt's smile quickly turned to an expression of panic as he realized he was on fire. Uncle Mike happened to be the closest in proximity to Matt and quickly threw his drink on him to extinguish the flames. Unfortunately, he was drinking whiskey, straight up.

Kelly knocked Matt to the ground and rolled him. She helped him pull off his burned coat. Matt looked at the damage. "Ekizian's Tuxedos is not going to be happy", Matt said still breathing heavily, sitting on his butt in the middle of the dance floor. Kelly smiled sweetly. "That's ok, Matt because Nick and Bill will be returning the tux and explaining what happened, right guys?" Nick and Bill nodded in agreement, happy that Kelly wasn't trying to kill them.

The rest of the evening passed in a happy, uneventful fashion. Kelly went to the bar to get a final glass of champagne. Nick sidled up next to her.

"Kelly, I'm so sorry. Are you gonna be mad at me forever?"

Nick looked a little worse for the wear, maybe three drinks past his limit.

"No, we're good Nick." Kelly leaned over and gave Nick a big hug. Nick hugged her back.

"I really hope that Matt knows he's the luckiest guy in the world, Kelly."

Kelly put her hand on Nicks chest and pushed away slightly to look up at his face. There was no trace of sarcasm there.

"Thank you, Nick," Kelly said, really touched.

"When he screws it up, and he will, Kelly, just remember, you can always come to me for comfort."

And just like that, Nick ruined the good feeling.

All of Nick's family members were lawyers or doctors. So when he announced that he wanted to be a school teacher, there were lots of mixed feelings on the subject. His father was annoyed. His mother, on the other hand was thrilled. Gina had always resented how much time Thomas had spent at the office. He'd missed so many school functions, little league games and dinners.

It wasn't as if they were struggling to pay the bills. They were both born wealthy, with huge trust funds, as was Nick. Nick was born with the proverbial silver spoon in his mouth. So Gina respected that he wasn't pretentious. Nick never tried to keep up with the Jones'. He marched to his own drummer. He didn't see why he was expected to go into a field he had no aptitude for, when he could teach and have summers off. He really enjoyed teaching, especially to children in Junior high. Not quite adults, but not babies either. It was fun to help them along and he liked their enthusiasm. Once they hit high school they were so self aware. It was fun to watch them start to experiment with their newfound freedom before they got all blasé about it in high school.

In the weeks and months that followed Matt and Kelly's wedding, Nick got up every day and went to work.

He showered, he ate enough to function, but he just couldn't gather enough enthusiasm to do anything with more than the minimum of effort. He stopped going to the gym, he ignored his friend's phone calls. He was unusually surly to students who were used to him being the cool teacher at school. His friends tried to give him some space and limit the calls but after three months they got nervous. They started to step up the phone calls and drop by with pizza or beers. They made him go to the gym. They called his sister Vicky who came over when Nick wasn't home and cleaned his house and opened up windows to air the place out.

After about a month of their combined efforts, Nick seemed to be getting a little bit better. He'd started to gain back the fifteen pounds he'd lost. He'd started to run again. He made an effort to entertain the children in his classes again.

A few months later, Bill Camden was getting married and Nick was in the wedding party. Bill was one of his oldest friends so he had to at least pretend to be enthused about it. They went to Atlantic City for the bachelor party. Matt was there and already complaining that married life was stifling him. Nick had to walk away from him before he killed him.

Nick proceeded to get very drunk and call Kelly to tell her he loved her. She replied, "Matt? Are you ok, you sound wasted. I love you too, honey, get some sleep." Nick hung up the hotel phone without correcting her.

Kelly called room service and ordered breakfast for three and two pots of coffee. There was no way she was taking Sam to the restaurant. In fact, she was seriously considering covering him with a blanket to smuggle him out of the hotel when they left. There was no telling how many people he pissed off last night in his Red Bull fueled rampage. She hung up with room service and turned around. Nick was staring at her from his position next to Sam on the bed.

"Too chicken to go down to breakfast, huh?" Kelly laughed.

"I prefer to think of it as self preservation, Nick. Just dodging the proverbial bullet."

Nick grabbed a bathroom towel and sunscreen off the dresser.

"Well, if it's ok with you, I think I'll go walk on the beach and maybe go for a swim and catch some sun until you're ready to go. Call my cell phone when Sam wakes up."

Nick spread his towel on the sand, took off his tee-shirt and ran down to the water and dove in. He swam for about 20 minutes and then walked back to his towel and decided to lay down for a couple of minutes. He contemplated putting on sunscreen, but it was hazy out. He let his mind drift instead.

He thought back to Kelly's wedding. He'd always wished he'd taken the chance and leveled with Kelly, not just about Matt cheating, but about his feelings for her. God, she'd looked beautiful on her wedding day.

Nick had watched Matt and Kelly say their vows, feeling sick to his stomach.

How had he let this happen? Why hadn't he stepped up that first day at the party before Matt had made a move? He had wanted to tell Kelly about Matt's cheating so many times, but there was no good way to do it without looking like a bitch. His fellow Groomsman, and close friend Bill put his arm around Nick's shoulder and squeezed in commiseration. Bill was the only person who knew how Nick felt about Kelly. Bill had talked Nick out of telling Kelly how he felt and what Matt had been up to. "You'll always be the guy who gave her the bad news bro," he'd said. Bill was right of course. Kelly wouldn't have thanked him for it.

Bill had also suspected that Nick's feelings for Kelly were what made her so attractive to Matt in the first place. Matt had always had an unhealthy competitive streak where Nick was concerned. Bill thought it was because things had always come easy for Nick. He came from a wealthy family, he was good looking, made honor roll without seeming to try.

Matt's family was middle class, he had to work at his grades and he'd always fought his weight. What made it worse was that Nick seemed to be oblivious to Matt's envy. Kelly wasn't even Matt's type. But if he had told Kelly she would never have spoken to Nick again and he'd have been in an even worse position. At least now Nick could try and be her friend and make sure Matt didn't screw it up too badly.

Except as time went by, Bill realized Nick couldn't make Matt treat Kelly any better as his wife than he had as a boyfriend. And poor Nick had never gotten over her. Bill had wished countless times that he'd told Kelly about Matt's cheating himself, that way Nick wouldn't have been the bad guy and she wouldn't have married Matt.

*T*wo years passed after Kelly and Matt's wedding and Nick was reasonably happy. He coached Little League and Pop Warner Football. He went to the gym and to work. He even went on the occasional date, but they never went anywhere. Nick just didn't find himself interested enough in anyone to try and pursue a relationship.

When he finally did meet someone, it happened quickly and without fanfare. Her name was Jillian Foster. Jillian was a twenty six year old accountant who lived in a rental house with four roommates. Nick had met her while waiting at motor vehicles to renew his license.

Jillian was 5'1" with dimples and chocolate colored eyes. Nick found himself smiling for the whole three hour wait. After they called his number and he'd concluded his business, Nick waited outside the front doors for Jillian to exit. When she spotted him leaning on the building her whole face lit up. Nick asked her out to dinner the following evening. Nick took her to his favorite Japanese restaurant. They talked for hours. Nick felt really at ease with Jillian. He wasn't in love, but it felt like it could be something close. Nick was twenty four years old and ready for a relationship. They filled the gaps for each other. They were each others dates to weddings, they went to the movies once a week, had dinner at each other's houses and slept together several times a week.

Jillian didn't make any demands on him. She was fun and upbeat. She knew how depressed he'd been when Kelly had married Matt. Bill had told her one night after they'd had one too many cocktails. They often ran into Kelly at mutual friends parties and while Nick did have a tendency to stare at her, Jillian tried not to let it bother her. After all, if she ran into an old flame she'd look too. That fact that Nick always seemed a bit down for a couple of weeks following a Kelly sighting was normal, wasn't it?

Nick was comfortable with Jillian but he just wasn't in love with her. For the first couple of years he had thought it was only a matter of time before he woke up one day and realized he wanted to spend the rest of his life with her. He kept waiting for it to happen but it never did. He didn't love her enough to take the next step.

Jillian on the other hand wanted more. She wanted Nick to finally commit to her. She was ready to start a family. They were compatible. So what if there were no sparks. She'd had the drama in other relationships and was glad there wasn't any in theirs. Jillian started to plan for the future. The more she talked, the more conflicted Nick became. They'd made no promises.

A couple of days before her birthday Jillian saw Nick leaving the mall with an adorable boxer puppy. She was so excited. She allowed herself to fantasize. She envisioned the puppy with a big red bow tied around its neck. It would walk towards her and there twined in the bow would be a robin's egg blue box. Nick would drop to one knee and ask, no beg her to marry him.

But her birthday came and went. Nick bought her a very pretty necklace, but no puppy, no diamond.

A few weeks later they were invited to a huge barbecue at Matt and Kelly's house. Nick looked preoccupied as he usually did around Kelly. Jillian was trying not to let it bother her when she spied a large puppy barreling out of the house. Kelly chased after it and picked it up. She laid it across her chest and nuzzled the puppy under her chin. Kelly walked over to Nick and Jillian and introduced them to the new addition to their family, Max.

Jillian sat quietly for the rest of the party. Nick was too preoccupied to even notice, which made the evening even more painful for her.

On the way home Jillian calmly turned to Nick and asked him if he'd bought the puppy for Kelly. He sighed and looked over at Jillian.

"Yes, but she thinks it's from Matt, Jillian. I didn't tell her it was from me. I just wanted to give her something to smile about for a change."

Jillian raised her eyes and looked at Nick sadly.

"What about me, Nick? Don't I deserve to smile?"

When they got back to Nick's house they sat and talked. Jillian told Nick she wanted to take the next step. Nick confessed he loved her but not enough to marry her. He wished he felt differently, but he just didn't. Jillian was heart broken, but deep down she wasn't surprised. She moved out two weeks later and Nick helped her move into her new apartment. They said they'd remain friends, but it was too hard.

Within a year Jillian was married to the love of her life, sparks and all. Nick received an invitation, but decided it would be too awkward. He sent the happy couple a two thousand dollar gift certificate for a pet store so they could choose their puppy together.

Chapter 12

Nick dozed off in the heat of the sun, with a cool breeze blowing the sand gently and the lulling sound of the waves hitting the shore.

He woke with a start when his cell phone rang.

"Hey Nick, we're ready to roll, whenever you get here."

Kelly sounded rested. Apparently Sam had slept until 1:00 pm.

"Sounds good Kelly. I'll head back now."

When Nick stood up and looked at his arms and legs he knew he was in trouble. He was lobster red already.

Nick got back to the hotel and ran into Uncle Mike who was in the process of checking out.

"Can you believe the cheek of these people? They just told me not to come back anytime soon! The nasty bastards."

Uncle Mike paused for breath and stared at Nick.

"Whoa laddy, forget the lotion, did you? Aunt Danis was just reading me one of them models tricks from her magazine. When they get too much sun they put hemorrhoid cream on it to ease the burning."

Nick looked dubious.

"Thanks Uncle Mike. I'll just help Kelly pack the car up and then I'll check and see if the gift shop has any in stock."

Sam and Kelly walked out of the elevator with the luggage.

"Hi Nick. I left your bag on the bed. We'll meet you at the car."

Kelly looked around for the manager, ready to dodge him and drag Sam with her. Sam ducked under Kelly's arm and ran towards the front desk. The woman working there screamed "stay back" and threw a complimentary pen at him. Nick ran over and picked Sam up, threw him over his shoulder, and walked Kelly to her car.

Once Kelly had Sam safely seat belted in she put the child lock on and told Nick to move his ass. Sam yelled out, "yeah, shake a tail feather lobster boy!"

Nick quickly ran to the room, took a thirty second shower and carefully dried off. He took a long look in the mirror and realized he was much redder than he had realized. His face was starting to ooze, which couldn't be good. I'll run in to the gift shop quickly and pick up that hemorrhoid cream, Nick decided. There was a tall, lanky teenager behind the register as Nick brought the preparation H up to be pay for it. The teen looked at the cream, stared at Nick's face and said, "Dude, hemorrhoids are the least of your problems."

When Nick got back to the car Kelly unlocked the door and Sam bolted out and ran to Uncle Mike.

"Can I ride with you, Uncle Mike? Please?"

Uncle Mike looked at Kelly and said as long as Kelly didn't mind.

"Uncle Mike, no more Red Bull, ok?"

Uncle Mike rolled his eyes. "It's a vitamin drink love. Stop being such a drama queen."

Kelly opened her mouth to protest and Nick put a hand on her arm and waggled his eye brows up and down.

"He's all yours, Uncle Mike," Nick said with a grin.

Kelly looked at Nick and started to laugh.

"That's really messed up Nick, poor Sam."

Kelly walked over and gave Sam a hug.

"Uncle Mike, Red Bull is an energy drink. Do not give Sam any, ok?"

"Nonsense Kelly, it's a vitamin drink. He'll be fine. He slept like a baby last night, not a peep, right Danis love?"

Kelly suspected them not hearing the commotion had more to do with the whiskey they drank. The only way Sam could have made more noise was if he'd blown up the room.

"Alright Uncle Mike, have it your way. We'll see you at home. Good luck"

Nick and Kelly loaded up the car and decided to hurry home to try and salvage the rest of the day before football practice started at 6:00pm. They kept the conversation light and opened the car windows and put the radio volume on high.

About an hour into the ride, Nick pulled into a pharmacy parking lot and Kelly ran in to get aloe lotion for his sunburn. Nick pulled his shirt off in the parking lot and let Kelly apply it to his back. She then made Nick take two aspirin for the pain and told him she'd drive the rest of the way home so he could nurse his sunburn. It was a beautiful day and the ride went by in a flash. As soon as Kelly pulled into the driveway she was up the steps dragging her bag behind her. Max bounded out of the house joyfully and leaped all over her. Nick offered to take him for a walk and Kelly almost cried she was so grateful. She hauled her bag into her room, threw herself face down on her beautiful new comforter and passed out cold.

Kelly woke up three hours later when her bedroom door was thrown open with a bang. Max leaped onto the bed and laid across Kelly's back.

"Forget something Kelly?" Peggy snarled from the doorway. "Your beast wouldn't let me out of the car. Why the hell would you let Uncle Mike give Sam a Red Bull? When I left the house he had already ran four miles on the treadmill. We had him running around the house at first but the neighbors were starting to gather to watch, so we brought him inside. Great job with your nephew. Good luck Max. I hope your mistress doesn't kill you!"

Kelly pushed Max aside and swung her legs to the floor.

"Peggy, I'm so sorry, I told Uncle Mike not to give him Red Bull."

Peggy cut Kelly off impatiently.

"Sam's in the bathroom. He's got football in an hour. I've got a car service picking me up for the airport tonight so Sam's staying here. Good luck with that. Try not to give him espresso or vodka as social services frowns on that."

Peggy threw Sam's overnight bag on the floor and headed out.

Kelly rolled over and put her head under the pillow. Sam strolled in and jumped onto the bed. He stuck his head under the pillow and gave Kelly a kiss on the cheek.

"I told Mom it wasn't your fault, Aunt Kelly. Is it ok if I go on the trampoline if Nick watches me?"

Kelly gave Sam a big hug. "No problem, Sam. Get hurt and I'll kill you and bury you in the backyard." Sam got up and gave Kelly his best reproachful stare.

"I am going to need so much therapy when I get older."

Kelly chuckled to herself. Sadly, he was probably right.

When Sam was six he'd asked her what gay meant. They were running late for school. Sam had five minutes to get to the bus stop so Kelly gave him a quick, off the cuff response, thinking she had years before she really had to get into this conversation with him.

"It means you like boys better than girls."

She'd gotten an irate phone call from Tim that night, asking why she'd told Sam he was gay. They'd sat Sam down and asked him if he wanted to marry a boy and he said no, but he didn't want to play with girls, just boys and Aunt Kelly said that made him gay. Kelly sighed. They'd given Sam a better explanation, Sam decided he wasn't gay, Tim was relieved and Aunt Kelly was told to direct further inquiries to Tim or Peggy. But the Red Bull was not her fault, damnit.

Jay's blog the next day read as follows;

"The Jersey Shore crew may have competition; look out Snookie, move over J Wow, we have a real situation here. The Red Bull fueled grandson of a pastry queen! But not to worry Jersey Shore crew, he won't be stealing your limelight, as he was asked not to visit again, anytime soon."

The Red Bull showed no sign of wearing off at football, even five hours after returning from the shore. Nick had the team run the track to warm up, with Sam in the lead.

When all the boys were sufficiently loosened up, he had half the team put on red jerseys. He had the defense try and crush the offense. Sam was running the ball for the offense and Nick was furious because his defense couldn't tackle him. He kept mumbling about sending out for a case of Red Bull for the rest of the team.

On Sam's last run with the ball he just kept going until he hit the track at the top of the hill. Nick was bellowing for Sam to come back as Kelly ran full speed to catch him before he made it to the parking lot. She tackled him just before he left the grass. It was a running tackle and they hit the ground hard.

As Kelly was trying to catch her breath and hold onto Sam, Nick yelled, "Now that's what I'm talking about! Kelly, show that to the boys one more time! Great job! You need to hit like that, gentlemen! Someone get Kelly a helmet!"

Kelly looked at Sam. The Red Bull was finally wearing off and Sam's eyes were already at half mast. She sat up painfully and grabbed Sam's hand.

"Come on buddy, you need to go to bed before you crash big time and I have to pitch a tent around you. There's no way I can carry you home."

Nick was still calling after them as they headed to the parking lot.

They dispensed with the shower, blew off brushing his teeth, and quickly pulled on pajamas. Sam was out cold before Kelly could pull the comforter up over his body. Kelly looked down at Sam's face. He was so cute when he was sleeping, so peaceful and angelic looking. Kelly snorted. She left the room quietly and clicked the door shut so Max couldn't get in and wake Sam up.

Kelly padded to the couch and lay down, covering herself with a fleece blanket. She woke up a couple of hours later and it was dark out. The clock read 10:15 pm. She went to her room and quietly put on an old tee shirt and flannel bottoms.

There was noise coming from the finished basement, but Kelly was too hungry to investigate what Nick was up to. Instead, she headed into the kitchen. She peered into the refrigerator and took out eggs, pepper jack cheese and turkey pepperoni. She diced up half an onion and some green pepper, sautéed it with a little butter and then assembled the rest of her omelet. Just as she was plating it Nick stuck his head into the kitchen. "Man that smells good! Any chance you'd be willing to share?"

Kelly grabbed another plate from the cabinet and slid half the omelet onto it. They took their food and headed downstairs to the rec room where Nick was busy watching football tapes in preparation for the next game. Jay and Abdul were playing Xbox and fighting.

"Hello Miss Kelly. Come and watch me kick Jay's butt."

Jay rolled his eyes. "Um, Abdul? I've won the last five games in a row. Time to throw in the towel, dumbass. No pun intended."

he doorbell rang and when Nick made no move to go and see who it was, Kelly walked up the steps, walked to the door and peered out through the peephole. Matt was standing on the door step with a huge bouquet of white roses. Kelly opened the door and stared at him.

"Hi Kelly, these are roses and me waving a white flag all at once," Matt said, waving the roses over his head. "Can we go for a drive and talk?"

Nick bounded up the stairs to get more beer for the guys and stopped short when he spotted Matt.

"Hi Matt, what's up?"

Matt smiled, "nothing much Nick. I just came by to talk to Kelly."

Nick looked at Kelly, who was looking distinctly uncomfortable.

"Well I don't think she wants to talk right now, Matt. You should call ahead next time."

Kelly stared at Matt. "Hold on Matt, let me get a sweater, it got cold out."

Kelly went to her room to retrieve it and Nick glared at Matt.

"What's your problem, Matt? Getting bored with gym girl and now you're back to bother Kelly? You're a selfish prick."

Kelly reappeared and Nick stalked past her.

"Get a grip Kelly. He doesn't have a loyal bone in his body."

Kelly looked at Matt. He looked shocked by Nick's outburst.

"Well? You wanted to talk so let's get this show on the road."

Kelly walked to Matt's BMW and got into the passenger seat and buckled up. As Matt pulled away from the curb, Kelly glanced back and saw Jay and Abdul standing on the front porch. Jay was pretending to choke himself.

It started to rain and Matt switched on the windshield wipers.

Kelly turned to face Matt. "What's this about Matt?"

Matt looked at Kelly and gave her his best winning smile. "I just wanted to talk about where we went wrong."

Kelly stared at Matt. "Well for one thing Matt you screwed around a lot. There was no "we" in that Matt, just you. We just didn't grow as a couple. We should never have gotten married to begin with."

Matt looked incredulous. "How can you say that, Kelly? We were great together. Aside from the Debbie thing, I was a good husband."

Kelly started to laugh. "Assuming that was true Matt, which is a huge assumption, what's the point of this conversation?"

Matt turned to Kelly, placed his hands on her shoulders and took a deep breath. "Ok Kelly, here it is. I'm sorry. I screwed up big time. It's time for you to come home. We need to get past this."

Kelly stared at Matt with her mouth hanging open. "This is bullshit Matt. What happened, gym girl went home to her parents? I have no intention of getting back together with you, ever. Pull over right now."

Matt had the nerve to look hurt, which infuriated Kelly even more.

"I can't believe you're being this cold Kelly. We had a life together, how can you just toss it aside?"

Kelly couldn't listen to him for another second. She hissed through clenched teeth, "If you're not going to pull over, then take me home right now, and please don't say another word."

Matt turned the car around in someone's driveway and headed back to Nick's house.

"I know you may need some time Kelly. I'm prepared to wait, for now."

Kelly shook her head. "Don't wait Matt. It's over."

Kelly got out of the car and ran up the front steps. Nick was sitting on the front porch with a bottle of Jack Daniels and Max was lying next to him. Both Max and Nick seemed to be glaring at her. Kelly went inside and closed the front door behind her. She dropped her wet jacket on the tile floor and padded to her bedroom. She flicked the light on. Sam was still out cold. She quickly put on dry pajamas and left the room. She lay down on the couch and went to sleep.

In her dream she was kissing Nick passionately and he was holding on to her tightly. She woke up with a start, to Nick actually kissing her. She'd responded in her sleep without waking.

"Don't do it Kelly. He's not the guy for you, he never was."

Nick covered Kelly with a blanket and kissed her forehead before walking away.

Matt was pissed. Nick should mind his frigging business. It was bad enough she was living under Nick's roof. If Matt was honest with himself, he did miss Kelly. He just hadn't realized how much until she moved in with Nick.

And if Nick had his way about it, she'd be moving into his bed also. Nick was always interfering.

Matt thought back to the sixth year he and Kelly were married. She wanted children and he told her he still wasn't ready. "Just give me a little more time Kelly. We have the rest of our lives to deal with rug rats."

Kelly had gotten the great idea to get a Boxer puppy she'd fallen in love with at the mall to assuage her maternal instincts. Matt had said no way. He didn't want to be tied down to anything but her. It was unusual for Kelly to fight him about anything, but she'd cried her eyes out about it. He'd bitched about it while playing basketball with the guys. Bill had told him to let her have the dog, what was the big deal. Nick remained silent, not commenting at all.

When Matt left for work the next day Kelly had taken a shower and was in the process of doing her hair when the doorbell rang. She opened the door and there was a dog cage on her front porch. Her baby boxer was inside with a big red bow around his little neck. She called Matt crying and telling him how much she loved him. What a great surprise it was. Matt had remained silent, seething. After Kelly stopped gushing, he choked out, "Anything for you, babe" and hung up the phone.

Matt never called Nick out about buying Kelly the puppy, wouldn't give him the satisfaction, but he hated that dog and Nick.

At every turn, Nick was there. Whenever he screwed up, Nick was watching. Matt got more blatant in his cheating. He started to rub Nick's nose in it, knowing there was nothing Nick could do. He remembered the first time he'd gotten caught cheating, how enraged Nick had been. Matt had loved rubbing his face in it.

It was their first anniversary and Kelly had taken the day off to clean the house. She'd made a trip to Dusty Rose lingerie and picked out a beautiful rose colored silk night gown with matching garters. Her next stop had been Laragia's cheese shop for some exotic cheeses and marinated olives. She'd picked up crusty loaves of Italian bread, expensive champagne and made a gourmet meal of filet mignon with brandy peppercorn sauce. She'd made white chocolate mousse with raspberries for dessert. She'd set the dining room table with an antique table cloth and broken out their beautiful wedding china. Waterford glasses sparkled. Kelly had lit dozens of tea lights and tapered candles. It really looked gorgeous.

Kelly had taken a long, luxurious bath and dressed in a very sexy low cut navy blue dress that she knew Matt loved. She'd bought an expensive pair of stiletto shoes that she'd probably never wear anywhere but in the bedroom, but they made her feel beautiful.

By 7:00 pm the seduction stage was all set and Kelly was excited for Matt to walk through the door. By eight he still wasn't home and Kelly called his cell phone. No answer. At nine she tried his office. Again, there was no answer. At 10:00 Kelly took off her dress and heels and put on a tee shirt and flannel pajama bottoms. She put a movie on and started to drink the champagne. Somehow the champagne wasn't working its magic and the pain in her stomach was getting worse. At midnight when Matt still hadn't materialized Kelly cracked and called Nick to see if he had any idea where Matt might be. Nick told her he hadn't heard from him.

The doorbell rang twenty minutes later and Kelly opened it with dread. It wasn't a police officer notifying her of an accident, thank God. It was Nick.

"Are you ok, Kelly?"

Nick looked at Kelly's stricken face and pulled her in for a hug.

"I don't know where he is Nick. It's our anniversary. I made dinner and waited. I keep calling but he's not answering. What if there's something wrong and he needs help?"

Not likely, Nick thought angrily.

"Don't worry Kelly, I'll find him. Go to the bathroom and wash your face. It'll be ok, I promise."

Kelly drew in a shaky breath and followed Nick's orders. As soon as she'd left the room Nick called Matt on his cell phone. Matt picked up on the first ring. Nick could hear female laughter in the background.

"Hey buddy, what's up? I'm at the clubhouse with Janine catching up. You should come hang out. Her friend Mimi is here. She's always had a thing for you. We were just about to leave and go back to her place."

Nick wanted to reach through the phone and choke Matt.

"Well for one thing asshole, it's your first anniversary and Kelly's been trying to reach you all night. She's losing it."

Matt groaned. "Oh shit, I forgot. I'll make it up to her another night when she calms down." Matt covered the mouth piece and yelled, "Be right there Janine."

Nick wanted to shove the phone down Matt's throat. "Nice one Matt. You really surpassed yourself this time. Not only do you forget your first anniversary, but you cheat on her too. I could kill you. I gotta go."

Nick closed his phone and turned to see Kelly staring at him.

"Oh shit Kelly, I'm so sorry."

He walked over and took Kelly in his arms. He hugged her tightly and kissed her forehead.

"Sit down and I'll get you a drink."

Kelly sat down on the couch looking stunned. Nick poured a huge glass of wine and handed it to her, sitting next to her on the couch. He pushed her hair off her face and kissed her. Kelly put her hand on his chest and pushed him away. She leaned forward, placed her glass on the table. Taking a deep breath, Kelly turned to Nick and kissed him. She felt a rush of passion more intense than anything she'd felt in her life. Without breaking the kiss they wrapped their arms around each other, afraid to let go or break the spell. They rolled to the floor and Kelly wrapped her legs around Nick's body. Nick started to pull Kelly's top off when the doorbell rang.

Kelly almost jumped out of her skin. She stood up shakily and straightened her clothes. She walked to the front door and threw it open. Her mother in law Kay stalked into the house.

"Has there been any word yet? How is he?"

Kelly covered her face. Her mother must have called Matt's mother. God knows I wouldn't call her, Kelly thought. Nick walked over and put his arm around Kay's massive shoulder.

"He's fine, Kay. He fell asleep on the office couch."

Kay looked Kelly over with contempt.

"My boy is working himself to death to keep you in the style you think you deserve and you have the nerve to embarrass him like this? Nice anniversary present Kelly."

She walked over to the table, sat down and helped herself to some chocolate mousse.

"I'll just wait until he comes home and have a word with him about your behavior," she said over a mouth full of mousse.

"I think you'll leave my home right now, Mrs. Chambers."

Kelly walked over, took the mousse out of Kay's hands and thumped it to the table. "Right now," Kelly repeated quietly.

Kay stood up to her full 5'11" and gave Kelly a withering look.

"At the very least you owe us all an apology you spoiled, little nobody."

Having said her piece, Kay stalked to the front door.

"I'll wait outside in my car for my son."

When the door closed, Kelly snickered. "I hope she brought a thermos and some blankets." Then she turned to Nick.

"I'm sorry for my behavior Nick. You better go home and get some sleep."

Nick searched Kelly's face but she'd retreated into herself again. Nick leaned forward and kissed Kelly's hair.

"Good luck, Kelly, I'll talk to you soon."

Kelly grabbed Nick's arm. "You're a great friend, Nick. I'm sure Matt will have a good explanation for this. Thanks for being there for me."

Nick got into his car, ignoring Kay who was gesturing for him to come and talk to her and pulled away from the curb. He drove to Janine's apartment and rang the bell until Matt answered the door in his boxers.

"What the hell's wrong with you, Nick? What couldn't wait until tomorrow?"

Nick grabbed Matt by his hair.

"Are you kidding me right now? What the hell is wrong with you?" he said knocking Matt's head against the door frame.

"Mind your own business, Nick. There's nothing you can do about it, so fuck off." Nick cocked his fist and punched Matt in the face and walked away disgusted. Matt fell to the floor.

"And don't go back to Kelly telling her stories, Nick. She'll always believe me anyway."

Matt went home the next day and told Kelly he'd tried to talk to Nick on the phone, but Nick kept jumping to crazy conclusions. He'd fallen down the stairs at work and knocked himself out, which is why the whole right side of his face was black and blue. According to Matt, the cleaning crew had found him on the ground, woke him and helped him to his car.

Matt surprised Kelly with tickets to Paris for a long romantic weekend to celebrate their first anniversary. He managed to convince her he'd never forget their anniversary. The fact that the tickets were booked after their anniversary registered in Kelly's mind but she chose to bury it in her subconscious.

Chapter 14

*M*att's surprise visit the night before had rattled Kelly more than she wanted to admit. She got up at the crack of dawn and went for a long run. When she got home after her run and still couldn't relax, she did a Pilates tape. That didn't help either, so the bathroom got cleaned, followed by the refrigerator. It was still only 9am. Kelly jumped in the shower, threw on jeans and a tee-shirt and headed to her mother's house.

Poppy Moriarty was thin and blond and could easily pass for her daughters much older sister. She had a dignified air about herself with an unexpected sense of humor that caught most people off guard.

She was very happy to see Kelly and threw her an apron.

"Idle hands, and all that, love. Have something to eat and then make yourself useful."

Kelly cautiously looked around.

"Don't worry, Uncle Mike and Aunt Danis went into the city today so they won't be stopping by, thank God. We have the house to ourselves. Grab an apricot tart and a mug of coffee and park yourself out of the way."

Kelly took a huge bite of the warm, fresh tart and sighed. She stared around at "Poppy's world" as Peggy and Kelly liked to call it. The entire huge kitchen was a spotless, state of the art masterpiece. Viking stoves, cooling racks, stainless steel and butcher block counters, and a huge double refrigerator. Poppy supplied baked confections to almost all the local restaurants and quite a few of the bakeries. Kelly took a big sip of her fragrant coffee. No one made coffee like Poppy.

"How's business, mom?"

Poppy eyed Kelly speculatively. "Why? Have you made a decision?"

Poppy had been begging Kelly to sell or close the costume store for years and become her partner. She needed the help. Her business had more than doubled in the last year.

"I'm leaning towards yes, mom. I think this will be my last Halloween and then I'll close shop. Does that work for you?"

Poppy clapped her hands and did a little dance of joy. "Right in time for the Christmas rush. Perfect! This calls for some Baileys! Irish champagne."

She got the bottle out of the frig and poured a large dollop in both their coffee mugs. Kelly was unusually quiet. She sat staring at her plate, breaking the tart into pieces, trying to formulate her question.

"Alright, out with it Kelly, what's got you looking so troubled?"

Kelly sighed, "Matt came by last night mom."

She explained what transpired to Poppy, trying to keep it brief.

"What should I do mom? Do I give it another chance? I told him no, buts it's ten years of my life. Am I wrong?"

Poppy stared at her daughter and walked over and sat down next to her.

"Kelly, I wish I'd given you a better life, more of an example of how not to be a door mat."

Kelly started to protest, but Poppy shushed her and continued.

"Things were not always pleasant here when you were younger. As he got older, your father calmed down, but he was always difficult. I put up with it because I loved him, but it was also because I had nowhere else to go, and he knew it. Things were different back then. There was no going home. My parents would have died of the shame. He cheated, he lied, he spent money we didn't have, and I made excuses for him. And you kids saw it all. I think you married Matt because he seemed easy going and fun. I don't think there was any real passion there. And I think his easy going personality was really indifference to anybody's feelings except his own. But he was drama free and that's what you were looking for. I taught you well," Poppy said ruefully. "I'm so very sorry. All my life I wanted peace and calm, but I also had passion with your father. It didn't make up for some of his more painful habits, but I knew why I loved him. When he died, I was heartbroken, but relieved. I was free to love him without the drama. I could do what I wanted for a change. I could live. I miss him every day but I'm glad to be off the roller coaster. Please Kelly, don't go back with him because it's easy. You'll always wonder when he's not home who he's with. That's no life either. And he'll always have an excuse for why you shouldn't have children and one day he'll come home and tell you he's gotten someone pregnant and it'll be too late for you to carry a child. You walked away already Kelly. Think long and hard before you walk backwards."

Kelly spent the next several hours happily baking and eating with Poppy. They reminisced about some of her father's more hair brained ideas, like cleaning the gutters with a hose attached to a rake, all the while perched on top of a ladder. Peggy and Kelly had run around underneath, ready to catch him when he fell, which of course he did. The hose had gone through the screen into the bedroom spraying everything in sight until they turned it off. Somehow all of Paddy Moriarty's ideas ended up causing the women in his life more work. A lot of his antics were entertaining, but too many were just painful to remember.

Kelly looked across the table at Poppy. "If you could do the day Dad came home with the motorcycle differently, would you Mom? What would you say?"

Poppy sighed "I don't know love. I don't think there was anything I could have done that would have changed things. He didn't ask for my opinion, he was too selfish for that. Even if I had taken the keys and thrown a fit he would have done what he wanted to do, and who he wanted to for that matter. I really truly loved him and it was never enough."

Kelly walked around the table and pulled a chair close to her Mom's and hugged her. "I love you, mom."

"I love you too sweetheart, and I loved your father. It wasn't that he didn't love me or you girls. He was just an insecure man who needed constant reassurance and it got exhausting. It's impossible to love someone day in and day out with the kind of intensity that'll convince them you mean it."

It was Thanksgiving weekend, three years earlier. Patrick had pulled onto their driveway on a motorcycle and Poppy was furious.

"Have you lost your geriatric marbles? We were supposed to be looking for a delivery truck for my business. You're too old to be riding that thing, Patrick. Please tell me you didn't buy it."

Patrick glared at Poppy.

"Don't worry, Poppy. I put a deposit on a delivery truck too. It'll be in in a couple of weeks. I just thought this was something for us, so we could live a little. Stop being so miserable. Why do you always have to rain on my parade?"

He got off the motorcycle, walked to Poppy and handed her a helmet. Poppy rolled her eyes and handed it back.

"Enjoy your toy Patrick, but if I didn't want to ride at twenty five, why would I now, at sixty."

Poppy shook her head and walked back into the house. Patrick got on the bike, strapped his helmet back on and drove away.

Patrick died six hours later, trying to avoid hitting a cat that had run into the road. He'd been all the way across town, going to see the *new girl* people had whispered in back of their hands with knowing looks and raised eyebrows.

The wake was a three ring circus. The rapscallion that he'd been, Patrick had friends from all walks of life. The only real commotion had come about on the second day when the local 45 boys had tried to take the casket out of the funeral home so Patrick could have one last drink at the Deer Head Inn. They'd been mollified when Poppy said they could share a drink with him in the funeral home. Father O'Keefe shrugged his shoulders and accepted the proffered plastic cup of whiskey good naturedly.

"If you can't beat them join them, eh Poppy?" Poppy nodded in agreement and took a sip from her cup.

Uncle Mike had stayed near the door both nights and Kelly had seen him hug a tiny blond and then turn her around and walk out to the parking lot with his arm wrapped around her shoulders.

Kelly had heard the rumors for years now. Every time her father got a new girlfriend the tongues started to wag as her Aunt Danis liked to say. But this was the first time

Kelly had actually seen one of her father's girl friends. They never lasted long. Once the woman realized Patrick wasn't going anywhere, that he truly loved Poppy in his own way, they usually gave up the fight.

The funeral was at ten am on a perfect fall day. It was sunny and unusually warm for the end of November. The Moriarty women sat together in the front row of the church holding hands. Poppy was exhausted and heartbroken. Deep down she knew none of this was her fault, but right now it didn't feel that way. The service was about to start when they heard a commotion coming from the doors of the church. Uncle Mike was arguing with the tiny blond he'd turned away from the wake. She was dressed head to toe in black and had on an overly dramatic black pill box hat with a little lace veil that covered her eyes. Kelly thought she'd definitely pushed the Jackie O look a little too far. Uncle Mike was exasperated and quickly losing patience. "This is pushing it too far Mindy. Have some decency and leave before the family sees you."

"I have a right to be here, Mike. He was a part of my life. I need to say goodbye."

Poppy got up from her seat in the pew and started to walk towards the commotion. Peggy tried to stop her mother, but Poppy told her not to make a scene and to please sit back down before people started to talk. Poppy strode quickly to the back of the church and grabbed Uncle Mikes arm.

"Michael, please sit down."

Uncle Mike started to argue, took one look at Poppy's face and did as he was told. Poppy took Mindy by the shoulders and hugged her. She grabbed her hand and walked back to the front of the church, Mindy in tow and sat back down. The service started without any more drama.

Chapter 15

*J*ay called and Kelly told him to come lend them a hand. Jay loved Poppy. He called her his steel shamrock. Poppy lost no time telling Jay about Matt's visit. Jay explained that he'd seen it with his own eyes and was appalled. He was even more horrified when Poppy told him Kelly was confused about what to do. Jay spent a full ten minutes pretending to kill himself, much to Poppy's amusement.

"Enough Kelly, for the love of God, the man's an ass hat, seriously. It's enough already. Think of your poor, ailing mother."

Poppy rolled her eyes.

Kelly laughed, "Alright, I get it. You've both made your point. Over, and over again, duly noted."

Matt called every day for the next several weeks. Kelly checked the caller ID and avoided answering when his name appeared. Nick took to leaving cryptic post its on her door. "Asshole called- Matt 1:00 pm." "Slow day at the gym- Matt 4:30." "Debbie at pre school, are you free for the next hour?-Matt."

The only time Matt managed to get her on the phone was at work where she couldn't ignore the calls. Kelly was polite, but adamant.

"You need to stop calling, Matt. I'm not interested and I need to get back to work."

Since the night Matt had stopped by Nick had been giving her the cold shoulder which was fine with Kelly. She was confused enough. There was an uncomfortable distance between them. They avoided each other as much as possible.

The Masonic Temple in Pearl River was hosting a huge Halloween Ball and Kelly was very busy. She had helped organize the party, as well as decorate and sell tickets. Anyone from the age of five and up were welcome to attend. It was the fifth annual party and Kelly's last. She'd decided that this was her last Halloween so everything was priced to sell. The closing date for the store was November Fifth and Kelly was very excited to start her new career with Poppy. If she somehow managed to survive this ball, that is.

Kelly was dressing as Tuesday from the Adams Family, complete with a headless doll and long black braids. Nick had purchased a pirate costume, and Sam was a tiny Casanova. Jay was coming as the Pied Piper. Angie had refused to dress up. She was wearing a name tag and carrying a perfume bottle. She was the perfume girl from Macy's, she told anyone who dared to ask. Peggy and Tim opted to go out to dinner and said they'd pick Sam up from the ball around ten pm before people got too inebriated.

The Hall was decorated with strings of orange and clear lights, crossed with black out lights which made anything white glow. Kelly had used all her accumulated decorations so that everywhere you looked there was something scary or entertaining. A headless horseman, Dracula, Frankenstein all held court. There were also several fog machines running at the same time which added to the eerie, festive atmosphere. There was a cash bar for the adults and tables loaded with cupcakes, candy and punch for the children. The DJ was playing great dance music and even people who normally stayed in their seats were hitting the dance floor as the drinks started to kick in. Sam was already out there swirling his cape and asking women as much as ten years his senior to dance. Jay was leading a conga line around the floor, pretending to play his flute the whole time, and unfortunately, Angie was finishing a huge solo cup overflowing with beer. Kelly tried to head her off, but Angie wouldn't listen.

"What the hell Kelly, if I can't be a psycho on Halloween when can I?" As a huge man in a diaper walked past them Angie tapped him on the shoulder.

"Perfume sample sir?" she asked sweetly and then without waiting for a reply squirted him right in the eyes. The guy screamed in a very unmanly way and ran for the men's room, presumably to throw water in his burning eyes. Kelly quickly walked away to see what Sam was up to. He was busy dancing with a middle aged Cinderella who was very entertained by her little Casanova. Kelly spotted Nick dancing with an Elvira. She felt her stomach twist a little and told herself she was being ridiculous. Why should she even care? He can do what he wants, she thought angrily. Elvira? Seriously, he couldn't pick someone with a little more imagination? Typical male. A large Peter Pan interrupted her negative train of thought and asked her to dance. Kelly downed the rest of her scotch and allowed herself to be led onto the crowded dance floor.

For the next 45 minutes Kelly gave herself over to the mix of great music and alcohol, laughing as Peter Pan, otherwise known as Phil spun and twirled her around the dance floor. For such a big guy, he was a surprisingly good dancer. Kelly finally pleaded exhaustion and headed to the ladies room. As she came out, Nick grabbed her around the waist and pushed her against the wall. He wrapped his arms around her pulling her close and kissed her passionately.

Kelly wanted to push him away, but felt herself respond to his kiss. Nick finally broke the kiss after a couple of minutes had passed.

"Peter Pan, Kelly, really? I would have thought you'd had enough of him by now."

Kelly picked up her headless doll and straightened her braids. Mind you own business Nick and stay away from me. Isn't Elvira waiting for you?" Kelly stormed off, furious that he'd gotten a rise out of her.

Angie was standing with Peter Pan Phil who was trying to rub the perfume out of his eyes. Kelly grabbed the perfume bottle from Angie and threw it in a garbage can. Then, she headed onto the dance floor to grab Sam who was dancing with a Tiny Cleopatra named Jordanna.

"Say goodbye Sam, it's time to go."

Sam looked at his Aunt like she'd lost her mind. "I'll go home when I'm ready woman," Sam growled at Kelly.

Kelly responded by grabbing Sam by his ear.

"Let go, I'm ready now. I'm ready now!" Kelly let go of his ear and Sam walked in front of her rubbing his ear and mumbling. "I'm not finding you very appealing right now Aunt Kelly." Kelly looked at Sam and laughed.

"I guess I'll just have to live with that Sam. Let's go."

Kelly rooted around in her hand bag and took her cell phone out. Peggy had left her a text message saying they'd be by in fifteen minutes to pick Sammy up. Kelly walked over to Angie and made her hand over her car keys. Then she told Jay she was leaving and asking Peggy and Tim for a ride home. Outside, Sam and Kelly sat on a wooden bench together and waited until Tim pulled up. Peggy looked very surly as she watched obviously inebriated people in costumes tripping over the curb.

Her mood didn't improve when Jay ran out waving to them and jumped in the car. "What's up Mr. Sister?" he bellowed at Peggy, causing Sam to laugh and choke on a cookie. Jay slapped him on the back repeatedly.

"Sam, stay away from the light!"

Sam laughed harder, leaned forward and threw up cookie on the floor of his mom's new Lexus.

Angie ran up to the driver's side window and tapped on the glass. Tim rolled down the window. "Perfume sample?" Angie asked sweetly and squirted him in the eyes. Tim howled in surprised pain and Sam doubled over laughing again.

Peggy bellowed, "That's it! Step away from the vehicle you little psycho!" She got out of the passenger's side and ran around to the driver's side, pushing Tim into the passenger's side.

"Get out, both of you, now!"

Jay whipped out his flute and said, "Come along Miss Kelly. The nights young and Peggy's not."

Kelly wiped Sam's mouth, made sure he was ok, and got out of the car. Peggy pulled out like a maniac, leaving the smell of burning tire in the air. Angie ran back into the party, perfume bottle in hand.

"Well, staying with Nick is probably looking like a good idea right about now, huh Kelly," Jay said, laughing. "Come along, let's check out the Shamrock Pub. With you dressed like that we should drink free all night."

The Shamrock was a seedy bar off the beaten path in Pearl River. It boasted a terrific juke box and surprisingly clean bathrooms. As usual, it was packed with a diverse age group and eclectic crowd. And by eclectic Kelly thought, I mean freaks. The bartender Will was a four hundred pound mountain of a man with a heavy Irish brogue and an amiable personality. There was an out of control rugby team downing boiler makers at one end of the bar and at the other end, Kelly's Aunt Danis and her cronies held court heckling the younger people and jeering at the rugby team whose record was less than stellar. Petey, the bouncer was eyeing the situation warily. Petey didn't look like much. He was 5'4" and slight, but he was a martial arts expert and kept things under control.

"Kelly love, come here," Aunt Danis shouted from across the bar.

One of the rugby players called out, "Kelly, don't go near them. They're spoiling for a fight, especially that trouble maker," he said, gesturing to Aunt Danis.

"Oh, shut your gob you poor excuse for a rugby player. Why don't you take up ballet?"

The rugby player looked at Kelly darkly and rolled his eyes. "Don't say I didn't warn you love."

Aunt Danis pounded on the bar. "A shot of Irish Mist for my Kelly, mountain man and make it snappy."

Will looked at Kelly pleadingly. "Please make her go home Kelly. She's driving me crazy. She keeps calling me fat boy. The rugby team wants to kill her. She's gonna get Petey killed and they gave poor Fergus a wedgie!"

Kelly looked at the eighty year old toothless Fergus propped up on the bar. Fergus nodded solemnly at Kelly, looking like he might shed a tear.

Kelly sighed. "I'll do my best Will." Kelly sighed again. So much for a peaceful drink, she thought darkly. She looked around to see where Jay had wandered off to. He was singing at the top of his lungs, surrounded by Aunt Danis's cohorts, none of them a day under sixty five. They were all swaying and singing to Tom Jones, "She's a Lady," while Jay did his best Tom impersonation. The oldest one of the group, at eighty six, Aggie Hanigan was fast asleep propped up in her bar stool, still clutching her shot glass. Kelly was pretty sure the biddies had broken her out of her nursing home for the evening. Kelly went to talk to Aunt Danis.

"Did you break Aggie out again without asking her daughter?"

Danis rolled her eyes dramatically and slapped her empty glass on the bar. "Her so called daughter won't even notice she's gone for at least a week, so get your knickers out of a twist Kelly."

Kelly took a deep breath and counted to ten. "How about I call Uncle Mike to pick you and the girls up or I can call a cab?"

Aunt Danis glared at Kelly. "I'm fine. If Will, the pretend Bartender would just do his job and stop whining like a fat girl at a candy store there'd be no problem!"

"That's it, you're cut off!" Will bellowed, slamming down a pint glass for emphasis.

Aggie, who had been sound asleep, was so startled she jumped off of her stool and glared around the bar. "Let the dog out yourself, old man," she screamed, throwing the shot glass across the bar where it hit poor Fergus in the forehead, knocking him off his stool and into the rugby players. The rugby players looked around in shock to see who had thrown something at old Fergus and saw Jay doubled over with laughter. The bar erupted in a huge brawl with rugby players and locals throwing punches at each other. Danis was pelting Will with coasters and he was busy deflecting them with a bar rag. Kelly grabbed her Aunt and dragged her outside. She called Uncle Mike and told him to get his ass down to the bar pronto to pick his wife up before the police got there or she was handing her over to them.

"Jesus, Kelly, Aunt Danis just likes a good ruckus, no need to threaten her with the coppers!"

Ten minutes later Uncle Mike pulled up and loaded Aunt Danis into the car. Petey carried Aggie out and put her in the front seat. Uncle Mike rolled down the automatic window.

"We'll have to talk about your priorities tomorrow Kelly. I'm very disappointed in you tonight young lady."

Without waiting for a response, he roared off in his caddy while Kelly stared after him with her mouth hanging open.

Kelly went back into the bar to grab Jay. Jay was standing on the pool table kicking anyone who got too close and poking people with a pool stick. Meanwhile the younger women from Aunt Danis's group were kicking and hitting the rugby players. Will was holding his head in his hands and had his elbows propped on the bar. He gave Kelly an, I told you so look. Petey was busy picking up old women and depositing them outside on the sidewalk, careful to lock the door on the way back in. Will had called the local cab company and three cabs had pulled up outside.

Will started buying beers for the rugby team which seemed to mollify them. They lost interest in Jay and walked back to the bar. Jay hopped off the pool table and with nervous looks at the rugby team, made his way over to Kelly.

"There's never a dull moment with the Moriarty family, eh Kelly? Boy, does your Mom owe me some baked goods, or what? This would have been headline news for me tomorrow. Maybe I'll go with the anonymous angle."

He adopted a fake British accent. "Which notorious local family took on an entire rugby team with nothing to "depends" on but the help of a niece?"

Jay cracked himself up. "Did you get the "depends" reference, you know, because of their age? Nice, right?"

Kelly glared at Jay. "Do it and die, Jay. Do it and die."

Jay smiled. "Ok Kelly, you win. I won't write about your Aunt."

Jay's blog the next morning was as follows;

"What trust fund pirate had a rest room rendezvous with a persnickety member of the Adams family who had to go home to make the donuts? And the inks not dry on this little cupcakes divorce papers yet! She better not act like a tart!"

Chapter 16

The Salvation Army picked up the last of the boxes and the extremely tired driver handed Kelly a receipt. Kelly looked around her at the empty store and sat down on the freshly vacuumed wall to wall carpeting. She laid all the way back, until she was staring at the ceiling. She stayed there making carpet angels with her arms and legs, too tired to get up. She'd opened her store on her fifth anniversary. Jay and Angie had helped her paint and Nick had set up the counters which had come unassembled. There was a huge back office that Kelly had planned to use as her packaging room. Most of her business was internet so she needed a lot of room to box up the costumes for UPS and FedEx. Nick had set up shelves and counters for her with their friend Bill Camden. Matt had called twice to let her know he was stuck at work, even though he'd promised to take the day off to help her.

Eight hours later, they were all sitting around a table eating Chinese food and drinking the champagne that Jay had contributed when Matt showed up. An exhausted Kelly waved to him and continued eating. Matt spotted Jay.

"Hey Janey, how's it hanging?"

Jay rolled his eyes. "Oh they're hanging great Matt, not as big as yours of course. I mean no one's balls are that big."

Nick choked on an eggroll and Angie slapped him on the back.

Angie glared at Matt.

"Great timing, Matt. You managed to get here when the work was done and the food arrived."

Matt laughed, "Some of us have real jobs Angie." He helped himself to an eggroll and headed to the front door. "I'm out of here, Kelly. Call me when your girlfriends leave."

He stalked out and was just getting into his car when Nick caught up with him. "Hold on Matt, where are you going?"

Matt glanced over his shoulder at Nick. "I'm going back to work, Nick. This is bullshit."

Nick looked in the driver's window at Matt. "Where were you really, Matt?"

Matt stared at Nick. "I was at work. Stop being an asshole."

Nick plucked a long red hair off of Matt's lapel.

"Really, Matt? Well tell work to stop leaving her cheap die job all over your suit." Nick dropped the stray hairs on the steering wheel.

"She's a coworker Nick. It must have gotten there when she walked by. Stop being such a woman. Tell Kelly I'll be home late."

Matt drove off, nearly clipping another car in his haste to get away.

The front door opened and Kelly quickly sat up. Matt strolled in. Just like five years earlier, he'd managed to avoid all the work. Matt looked around and whistled. "Wow. You really got a lot done. It must be a relief to be closing up this place, huh Kelly?"

Kelly looked up at him and smiled sadly. "You never did get it Matt. It was a lot of fun while it lasted. I just want to do something else now. My mom needs me and I'm looking forward to working with her. I managed to sell the internet side of the business, so it was all worth it in the end."

Matt shook his head and laughed. "Well, whatever makes you happy, Kelly. Now that you've got this taken care of, why don't you come home? I miss you."

Matt reached down and helped Kelly to her feet. He pulled her close and hugged her.

"At least let me come for Thanksgiving and spend some time with the family. We can get past this."

Kelly broke the news that Matt would be joining them to her assembled family and friends as they were setting the dinner table. Angie stomped out of the room.

"Well, if that dick is coming, I'm drinking," she announced, pouring herself a chocolate martini from an icy pitcher.

Angie had brought Eddy with her and he was just finishing folding the cloth napkins in the special way Poppy had shown him. The rest of Angie's family was coming for dessert after visiting Bella in the psychiatric center. Poppy finished setting the table, putting the huge Thanksgiving bouquet in the center. Matt had sent it earlier in the week, no doubt hoping it would soften Poppy's heart. It didn't.

"Kelly love, bring out the appetizers. Angie, put down that martini before I slap you."

Angie rolled her eyes at Poppy.

"Right now, young lady," Poppy hissed from between clenched teeth.

The doorbell rang and Poppy greeted Peggy, Tim, and Sam. A few minutes passed and Uncle Mike and Aunt Danis arrived with, smoking Mo, As the Moriarty's were now calling Maureen. Poppy dragged Sam off to the kitchen to help and Maureen trailed behind, happy to be doing whatever Sam was doing. Uncle Mike headed right to the liquor cabinet and poured himself a whiskey, neat.

"So, I hear young Matt the philanderer will be joining us? Good! Aunt Danis has a few things she'd like to discuss with him. I assume he won't be bringing the young floozy?"

Angie laughed gleefully. "And you were worried about me putting my foot in my mouth? It appears I'm the least of your problems."

Kelly plunked the bowl of cranberry sauce she was carrying down with a thump, rattling the beautiful crystal and china and getting everyone's attention.

"No one will embarrass me tonight. Do you hear me, you bunch of lunatics?"

They all started to argue at once.

Poppy clapped her hands over her head.

"Anyone who embarrasses Kelly will have to answer to me, have I made myself clear?" Poppy glared around the room. Everyone, including Uncle Mike nodded and promised to behave.

Matt arrived a half hour later to a strangely subdued Moriarty clan. Sam gave Matt a big hug and Kelly exhaled in relief. Her relief proved premature when she heard Sam ask, "Uncle Matt, what's a philandering Tom Cat?"

All in all, the evening turned out reasonably pleasant. Matt was at his most charming and everyone warmed up quickly, with the exception of Poppy. The more everyone seemed to enjoy Matt's company, the surlier Poppy became. By the time the cherry cobbler and after dinner drinks were served, Poppy was practically foaming at the mouth.

Matt helped to clear the rest of the dessert plates and said his goodbyes. When he got to Poppy he stopped and grabbed her hands.

"Mom, I hope you're able to forgive me some day."

Poppy looked Matt straight in the eye. "Not likely, Matt. I know a snake when I see one. I wish you well, but not with my daughter. You blew it."

Matt was so shocked he was literally speechless. He nodded at Poppy as if to say "fair enough" and walked out the front door.

"Goodbye, snake," Eddy yelled after Matt, waving cheerfully.

Kelly walked Matt to his car and gave him a hug.

"She'll come around Kelly, you'll see."

Kelly looked up at Matt. "How do you know that, Matt? I'm not even sure that I'm going to come around." Matt laughed.

"Of course you will Kelly. I'll call you during the week, unless you want to come back to our house for old time's sake tonight?" Kelly shook her head.

Matt sighed. "Fine, Kelly. I'll call you during the week."

He walked around the front of the car, got in and beeped the horn twice. Kelly watched as he drove away. She walked back into the house and Poppy called out to her from the kitchen. Kelly walked past the family room where everyone was groggily watching a football game. Angie mouthed "good luck." Poppy was just stacking the last of the dishes. She poured two glasses of brandy and handed one to Kelly.

"Sit down love." She looked at Kelly sadly.

"Kelly, I had nowhere to go love, you do. You've got a lucrative job and a family. Enough is enough. Matt is just your father in sheep's skin. At least your father wasn't a sneaky bastard. Stop pretending Matt is someone he's never going to be. Now what about that lovely Nick? He's someone worth getting fired up about."

It was Thanksgiving three years earlier. The whole family was gathered at Uncle Mike and Aunt Danis' house. Matt got held over on business and said he would try to get there in time for dessert.

The day went on and on and Kelly still hadn't heard from him. Every time she tried his cell phone it went directly to voice mail. Finally, it was time to go home and Kelly said her goodbyes, glad to be getting away from the inquisitive looks of her relatives. On the way home her father kept staring at her in the rearview mirror.

"I'm sure he's fine, Kelly. Why don't you spend the night with us?"

Kelly was really tempted, but just wanted to climb into her own bed and go to sleep. The thought of climbing into the lumpy twin bed of her youth was just not appealing. Her father pulled his car into her driveway ten minutes later. Matt's car was there.

"See there Kelly, he must have just got home. Sleep well and call us tomorrow." Kelly thanked her parents, ignoring the looks they were exchanging with each other. She walked up the porch steps and let herself in with her key.

Matt was just coming out of the bathroom, fresh from the shower, still in the process of toweling his hair dry.

"How's the family, Kelly? Any good brawls?"

Kelly sat down at the kitchen table and sighed. "How come you didn't show up, Matt?"

Matt stared at Kelly in exaggerated annoyance. "I just walked in Kelly. Give me a break. I did the best I could. I've got to get some sleep. We can talk about this tomorrow."

Kelly went into the living room and sat on the chaise lounge, trying to calm herself down from the anger that was threatening to break loose. At the very least he could have answered his phone or apologized.

The house phone rang and Kelly ignored it, letting the answering machine pick up. An unfamiliar voice came through loud and clear from the kitchen machine. "Hello, this message is for Mr. Chambers. This is Paul from the Hungry Lion Restaurant calling. You and your wife were in earlier this evening? You left your credit card on the table sir. We can hold it here for you or drop it in the mail. Just give me a call and let me know what you want me to do. Have a nice evening."

Kelly got up off the couch, grabbed her coat and purse and headed out the front door. She walked ten blocks until she reached the nearest bar, The Clarksville Inn. The juke box was blaring and despite the smoking ban, the bar was filled with a smoky haze. Kelly snagged a seat at the bar and promptly ordered a martini, instructing the bartender to keep them coming. Kelly had just finished her third drink when Nick sat down next to her.

"Kells bells, what brings you out tonight?"

Kelly rolled her eyes and turned to look at Nick. "Nick, please put a cork in it, ok? I'm so not in the mood for what you think passes as witty banter."

Nick opened his mouth to respond but decided against it when he took a good look at Kelly's face. Instead he called out to the bartender.

"Kevin, I'll have whatever this gorgeous lady is drinking."

When Kevin had put the icy martini glass in front of him and he'd taken a huge slug, he turned and faced Kelly.

"Alright, out with it. What happened?"

Kelly looked down into her drink and muttered softly, "How long has Matt been cheating on me, Nick?"

Nick sat back heavily in the barstool and ran a hand through his hair.

"Oh shit, Kelly. Even if he was, he sure as hell wouldn't tell me. Why, what happened?"

Kelly shook her head. "Just drink with me Nick. I really don't feel up to talking about it. He's been fooling around for years and I pretended it wasn't happening. You knew. Don't lie to me. Don't you dare lie to me."

Nick looked at Kelly angrily. "I'm not lying Kelly. He doesn't tell me who he's screwing. He knows how I feel about you. It's been a long time since Matt and I confided in each other."

Kelly put her hand up to Nick's mouth.

"Please stop talking. If you're going to stay next to me start drinking, otherwise find someone else to annoy."

Nick shrugged and called out to Kevin, "shots of Jamison's and keep them coming Kevin. It's gonna be a long night my friend."

Three hours later Kelly was crying in her beer, almost incoherently. Nick threw money on the bar, said good night to Kevin and helped Kelly out to the waiting cab. He made sure her seatbelt was on and gave the driver her address. Kelly put her head on his shoulder.

"You're a good friend, Nick. I bet you wouldn't cheat on me. Never mind, you probably would."

Nick grabbed Kelly's chin and forced her to look at him.

"I would never cheat on you, Kelly. Never," Nick said emphatically. "I love you and one of these days you'll figure out you love me too."

Kelly leaned forward and kissed Nick. "Take me home with you. I need to sleep on your couch."

Nick shook his head. "If you come home with me, Kelly, you're not sleeping on the couch."

Kelly nodded her consent and Nick told the cab driver there was a change of plans and gave him his address. The cab driver, whose name was Abdul, smiled and made a u turn. Two minutes later Kelly was snoring on Nick's shoulder. Nick cursed under his breath and said "Hey, Abdul." Abdul looked at Nick and the sleeping Kelly in his rear view mirror.

"I know. I know. Change of plans. What address would you like me to take you to now?"

By the time the cab pulled up in front of Peggy's house, Kelly was a boneless mess. It took Nick ten minutes to get her out of the cab. He had to carry her to the front door and propped her up while he rang the bell. Tim threw open the front door, looking from Nick to Kelly in confusion. He'd just woken up and was having trouble processing the situation, due to exhaustion.

"What's going on Nick? What happened?"

Nick whispered to Tim. "She's had a little too much to drink Tim. She needs to sleep it off on your couch."

Tim padded towards the kitchen, looking back at Nick.

"I'll call Matt."

Nick shook his head. "Don't Tim. Kelly found out he's cheating again."

Tim turned fully and stared at Nick. He exhaled loudly and raked both his hands through his hair, making it stand on end.

"She needs to lose that asshole Nick. I know he's your friend but he's a dick." Nick carried Kelly over to the couch and laid her down, turning her sideways in case she threw up during the night. He grabbed a throw off the back of the couch and draped it over Kelly. He stood up and looked at Tim and sighed.

"Do you really think I don't know that Tim? He's always been a dick with women. He loves Kelly but he's not going to change. Nothing will change until Kelly leaves him. Do me a favor, just check on Kelly during the night and make sure she's ok." With one last glance at Kelly, Nick turned around and headed out to the cab, closing the front door behind him.

Tim locked the front door, turned off the lights and headed upstairs to let Peggy know what was going on. Time to visit the home office for a couple of days, Tim thought, shaking his head.

Chapter 17

*K*elly pulled into Nick's driveway and shut the car off. She was absolutely exhausted. She dragged herself to the front door and fumbled with her key, too tired to get it into the lock properly. She finally pushed the door open to find Max passed out cold in the hallway.

"You are some kick ass watch dog, you big slug." Max didn't even open his eyes.

Nick had left a note taped to the hallway mirror.

"Hey Kelly, If you're reading this something has gone horribly wrong. No, just kidding. I always wanted to say that, lol." Kelly rolled her eyes and kept reading. "I took Max for a six mile run so he should be good until tomorrow morning, especially since I carried him the last mile. He was pretty wiped. I'm staying at my parent's house until Sunday so have fun and water the plants. No, don't, they're fake. No Keg parties while I'm gone, your friend and future lover, Nick." Kelly sighed. Stepping over Max, she headed to the bathroom and took off her makeup. She padded to the kitchen and grabbed a bottle of water from the fridge.

Her cell phone rang and she answered after checking to make sure it wasn't Matt. As soon as Kelly said hello, Jay started talking.

"What's up, my fickle friend? Let me ask you something. Does your family ever casually ask if you play for the other team?" Jay asked.

Kelly choked on her water and started to laugh.

"No? I didn't think so. The worst part was that I thought they were talking about my Sunday softball league. I think the only way I'll ever convince my loved ones that I'm not gay is to have sex on the dining room table while they're having dessert. Don't worry about baking, Mom. I'll bring a tart, ha ha. Anyway, enough about my cave family, what are you doing, and please don't say Matt."

Kelly put a bottle of white wine in the freezer.

"Nick is gone until Sunday. Are you up for a pajama party?"

Jay dropped the phone with a clatter. Kelly could hear his voice in the background. "I'm just packing a few things. See you in half an hour. Call Angie and tell her I'll pick her up on the way. We'll make her drink and let the shit hit the fan."

Three hours and many drinks later Jay talked them into going on a bar crawl in Nyack. He was attempting to do Angie's hair and makeup. Kelly had put on a very flattering navy dress with a plunging neck line. She was rummaging through her closet trying to find something that wouldn't swim on Angie. She finally found a stretchy black dress that still had the tags on it. Kelly had bought it at a designer tag sale and swore she would diet into it. Since it was a size two, it never actually happened. She held it up and admired the sparkly pattern and ribbing thru the bodice.

"Come on, throw it this way sister. You've had that for two years. If you haven't gotten into it by now, you ain't ever getting into it," Jay said laughing.

Kelly gave him a dirty look and threw it to him.

"Rub it in, why don't you. Easy for you two, but some of us like to eat."

Jay looked her up and down. "It looks good on you Kelly. Besides, not everyone can have my stellar metabolism."

"Hold still Angie or I'll slap you with the brush. I swear it's like trying to put makeup on an angry raccoon," Jay sniped. As quickly as Jay was applying it, Angie was wiping it off. Jay handed the dress to Angie and she held it up to scrutinize it. Angie looked down at what she was wearing, old Levis, biker boots, and a tank with an old flannel shirt and knew she wasn't going to win this argument. Sighing, she stripped off her top and pulled the dress over her head.

"Fine, I'll wear the dress, but the boots stay on."

Jay looked her over from head to toe and laughed.

"On you Angie, the boots work."

Twenty minutes later, Abdul's cab pulled up.

"Oh Goody," he exclaimed, "the little one's drinking," he said glancing at Angie. "Can we swing by my house for the video camera?" he said hopefully.

Kelly started to answer, but Jay cut her off.

"Absolutely Abdul, just as soon as pigs fly out of my ass. Now drive the damn cab, man." Jay laughed at Abdul's hurt face.

Abdul scowled at Jay and addressed Kelly.

"Where to tonight, Miss Kelly?"

Kelly told him to take them to O'Doul's Bar in Nyack. Still scowling at Jay in the rearview mirror, Abdul pulled out of the driveway and headed towards Nyack.

O'Doul's Bar was packed and Angie was fuming.

"You can't swing a dead cat in this place without hitting a cop or a fireman."

Jay rolled his eyes. "Sorry Angie, but the Goth bar and grill (stake, anyone?), required a blood donation to get in. You'll just have to make do with the blue collar crowd."

Angie smirked at him. "Shut your pie hole, Jay. Hey…I know. The Coven Café sponsors a woman's softball team. Who knows? Your future wife could be there right now drinking a Budweiser! Hurry Jay. Let's not waste another moment. Finish your drink, she's waiting for you."

Jay stared at Kelly morosely. "This is shaping up to be a long night."

They drank their way up the block, stopping once to watch Angie eat five slices of pizza without coming up for air. Kelly shook her head.

"Now that just pisses me off. Not an ounce of fat on her. How is that fair?"

Walsh's Bar and Grill was equally packed but they managed to get three seats at the bar. They were there maybe five minutes before Angie started to harass Greg the bartender. When he got to the point where he looked like he was going to break something, Angie batted her eyelashes at him.

"I know you're just dying to ask me out, right Greg?"

Without missing a beat Greg shot back, "You're right, I am. Get out."

Kelly begged him not to throw Angie out, and after leaving him a healthy tip, Greg agreed to let her stay.

After a few more rounds of drinks, Kelly noticed a guy at the other end of the bar staring at her. He looked vaguely familiar and as she was trying to place where she knew him from he got up and headed in her direction. To her horror and mortification, she realized it was Al Pacino.

When he got about one foot from her he bellowed, "I can too handle the truth lady! Jack Nicholson can't. I just can't stand being misquoted, Missy. Next time, bone up on your trivia before you show up on my doorstep. Dumb-ass."

Jay snorted beer out his nose, all over Angie, who punched him so hard he fell into Kelly, who in turn fell over, bar stool and all, onto Mr. Pacino's foot.

As Mr. Pacino was being loaded into the ambulance, the star struck medic, clearly a huge fan looked at him, stood up and loudly quoted, "You're out of order, this whole trial is out of order!"

Kelly shook her head sadly at the medic and smiled condescendingly. "Nice try, but that's Jack Nicholson, not Mr. Pacino."

Mr. Pacino reacted by taking his shoe that the para-medic had already removed and throwing it in Kelly's direction. It nailed Jay square in the forehead.

Kelly wanted to accompany Mr. Pacino to the hospital, but he requested that she get the hell away from him. Thankfully, seeing that it was an accident, Mr. Pacino declined to press charges. Nyack Hospital put a cast on his foot and an ice pack on Jay's forehead and sent them home.

The next day an anonymous package arrived with all of Al Pacino's movies. The attached note read, "Watch them dumbass."

Kelly was strangely touched and reciprocated by send-ing a huge basket of her most popular baked goods, beau-tifully wrapped with Poppy's signature dotted cellophane and the complete works of Jack Nicholson on DVD.

Mr. Pacino liked Poppy's baked goods so much that he requested that his movie crew use her to cater their film location's coffee breaks. He personally called Poppy to let her know. After talking for half an hour on the phone he invited Poppy to come visit the movie set, but requested she not bring Kelly as his insurance company couldn't han-dle any problems that she may inadvertently cause. He had a car come and pick Poppy up for the visit and after the driver had helped Poppy into the car, he popped the trunk, removed the Jack Nicholson movies and put them on the front porch.

Saturday night they decided they were too wiped out to hit any local bars so they had a nice relaxing dinner at a Mexican restaurant in the Palisades Mall, washed it down with margaritas and went to an early movie. The only tense moment was when Angie threw a milk dud at the back of a very large obnoxious man's head after he talked for ten minutes on his cell phone during the movie. He jumped out of his seat and glared around the crowded theater, but nobody threw Angie under the bus so he let everyone know they were on notice for an ass kicking and sat back down. Kelly had to leave to go to the ladies room until she could stop laughing.

When they finally got back to Kelly's, the phone was ringing off the hook. After first checking the caller ID to make sure it wasn't Matt, Kelly saw Peggy's cell phone number and picked up.

"Why couldn't you watch Sam for the night, Kelly, why?"

Kelly sighed. "What happened, Peggy? Is he ok?"

Peggy snorted. "I need you to go pick him up from Uncle Mike's house. Let Aunt Danis tell you what happened."

Jay pulled his car into her Aunt and Uncle's driveway and parked behind their huge Lincoln.

"Do you want me to accompany you in or stay put," Jay said hoping for the latter.

Kelly pushed her hair off her face and laughed. "No Jay. You better go home. This may get ugly and I wouldn't want you to take any shrapnel."

Kelly walked into the fancy living room with its fussy arm doilies and Aunt Danis leapt up from her chair.

"It wasn't a big deal, Kelly. Just a couple of boys having some fun. The coppers always overreact, don't they now. Care for a cup of tea, love?"

Kelly walked across the room and sat down in Uncle Mike's overstuffed recliner. "What happened?" she asked sinking further into the cushions.

Aunt Danis rolled her eyes. "The boys walked into town to see a movie. On the way home they pass old Ella Fitzpatrick's house, the one with all the garden gnomes. Well Sammy thought it would be a laugh to put the really large one on the porch with all the smaller ones lined up at the bottom of the steps facing him, like he'd called them to a meeting. Then Uncle Mike rang the doorbell and ran away and they hid behind a bush to see Ella's face when she opened the door. Well the plan worked pretty well," Danis said proudly. "They scared the beJesus out of poor, old Ella. Sam said she jumped about four feet into the air. Unfortunately, when she came down she missed the first step and rolled down the rest. There were gnomes flying everywhere. Honestly, it wasn't that big of a deal. The hospital said she'll be fine. The nurses gave her something for the shock. She only bruised a couple of ribs and fractured a toe or two. Uncle Mike got a disorderly conduct ticket and one for trespassing. Sam has to miss his next football game and take care of old Ella's yard work for the next month or until her ribs heal. Plus, she'd like the gnomes removed. Turns out they were husbands and they scare the hell out of her. So there you go! We've actually done her a favor."

Kelly stared at her Aunt.

"Really Kelly, Ella's fine now on account of the case of Jamison's I brought to her house. She's even dropped the charges. The nurses at the ER told her how you broke Mr. Pacino's foot so she feels like she got off easy. So, all's well that ends well, eh Kelly love?"

Uncle Mike came barreling into the room.

"For the love of God, Kelly, don't make a mountain out of a mole hill. All boys are bad! Why, even Jesus was a rascal."

Kelly just stared at her uncle. Uncle Mike nodded knowingly.

"Where do you think the expression "Jesus Christ" came from? Or how about, "Mary Mother of God?" It was probably, "Jesus Christ! Mary Mother of God, will you look at what your son's done now? He's turned all the damn water to wine again, and what the hell am I supposed to do with all these fish!"

Kelly didn't even bother to respond. Instead, she turned and addressed her Aunt.

Kelly smiled sweetly at Aunt Danis. "Sure, it's not a problem at all! Sounds like just a bit of fun amongst the boys."

Uncle Mike started to nod enthusiastically until he saw the look on Kelly's face. "Now go ahead and call Nick. Let him know why Sam won't be playing football this Sunday. Let's see how much fun that conversation is, because I sure as hell won't make the call!"

Kelly clicked on Jay's blog fearfully. It was asking too much for him not to have posted after this weekend. Sure enough, he'd made sure to post it.

"What notorious philandering cheapskate talked his soon to be ex wife into letting him scarf down a free Thanksgiving dinner? Wake up, jack wagon, this cupcakes not taking you back, stick with the tart. Also in local news, there was a gnome summit meeting that was apparently unscheduled, wreaking havoc on a poor, unsuspecting, elderly lady, who shall remain nameless. It also sidelined a local football youth for at least one game. Fortunately, those gnomes know how to make amends. Its true folks, Jamison's does cure all ailments. FYI, the gnomes are now residing on the philandering cheapskates front lawn, thanks to yours truly, so ladies beware, there's gnome relationship worth pursuing there. Take it from the cupcake, who may soon be residing in Attica! Attica!"

Chapter 18

*N*ick pulled into the driveway, Kelly and Sam in tow.

"I leave for one weekend and the lunatics are running the asylum."

He turned the car off and headed into the house, turning to glare at Sam.

"This really sucks, Sam. What were you thinking? Go to bed, we'll talk tomorrow."

Sam slouched out of the room looking dejected. Nick rounded on Kelly, looking her up and down disdainfully. Before he could deliver whatever scathing remark he had in mind, Sam called out to Kelly.

"Aunt Kelly, could you kiss me good night please?"

Saved by the little gremlin thought Kelly as she told Nick to hold that thought and ran from the room.

Sam was curled up under Kelly's six hundred thread count Egyptian comforter. "I'm really sorry, Aunt Kelly. Nick looks pretty mad, huh? I guess I'll be running laps for the whole game tomorrow. I should have waited for you before I pulled operation gnome. We wouldn't have gotten caught."

Kelly looked at Sam's mischievous face and cracked up.

"Sammy, never get Uncle Mike involved in any prank. He will always screw it up."

Sam rolled his eyes. "Ya think, Aunt Kelly?"

Kelly smiled. "Old Ella has her faults, but she was very nice under the circumstances. I'll have Grandma bring her over a huge gourmet basket tomorrow."

Sam gave Kelly a doubtful look. "I think Aunt Danis had the right idea with the whiskey, Aunt Kelly, no offense. Thanks for asking Nick to go easy on me," he said, looking up at Kelly from under his eyelashes, big brown eyes twinkling.

"Mom told Dad you should take one for the team since it was your fault I was at Uncle Mike's in the first place. Goodnight Aunt Kelly. I love you."

Sam closed his eyes and burrowed under the comforter and within seconds he was asleep, his breathing slow and soft, looking more like an angel than the rascal he was.

Kelly sighed and stood up to leave the room. Time to face the music, she thought ruefully.

Kelly tip toed out to the kitchen. Nick had lit a candle and put a platter of cheese and crackers on the table. Kelly stopped short and stared. Nick turned from the kitchen counter holding two drinks in his hands and laughed when he saw Kelly's expression of mistrust.

"Come on Kelly. You'll have a drink with everyone else, but not me?"

Kelly smiled and took the proffered drink gratefully. She sat down at the kitchen table and stared at the cheese platter to avoid making eye contact with Nick. Staring up at her from the middle of the platter was a tiny gnome. Kelly burst out laughing and looked up at Nick. Nick smiled and shook his head.

"I will never understand how your Uncle has avoided doing jail time."

Kelly laughed harder. "That makes two of us Nick. Remember the time he tried to blow up his car for the insurance money but first he used the car to drop Aunt Danis and the biddies to the bar and came in with them to grab a handful of match books?"

Nick snorted. "But his real mistake was buying lighter fluid on the way to the bar. In January. How he got out of that one, I'll never know."

Nick laughed and stood to refill Kelly's martini glass. He filled both of their glasses and pulled his chair closer to Kelly's.

Kelly was very aware of Nick's close proximity and wished she wasn't so affected by it. He smelled like musk, mixed with fresh air.

"So Kelly, how do you think I should handle the Sam versus the gnomes' incident," Nick said playfully, his thick lashed eyes taking on a mischievous look.

Kelly looked up at Nick and laughed. "Well, Sam said I should take one for the team. But I think he's giving me way too much credit."

Nick pulled Kelly's chair closer and pulled her onto his lap, gathering her hair off of her face and exposing her neck.

"No, he isn't, Kelly."

He kissed her neck and then turned her face towards his. He kissed her and she wondered why she'd ever tried to fight it. They stayed that way for a long time until Nick half carried, half dragged her to his room. Locking the door behind them, they fell to the bed. Long years of trying to pretend she wasn't attracted to Nick fell by the wayside as she finally just let her emotions take over.

Kelly woke up in the early morning hours to the sound of Max head butting the door. She slid from under the covers and opened the door so he could come bounding joyfully into the room. Nick jumped up and closed the door.

"Oh, no you don't Kelly. Sam won't be up for at least two hours. You still have quite a bit of debt to pay off in his defense." He pushed Kelly back into bed and proceeded to collect.

Kelly dragged herself out of bed two hours later and made a pot of coffee. Nick had already put bacon in a frying pan and was making pancakes. He stopped cooking long enough to pour Kelly a huge coffee, loaded with sugar and cream, the way she liked it. She sat at the table watching Nick cook and reliving the night. It was better than she ever hoped to imagine it would be. Nick was generous in bed in a way Matt never was. He also knew the way she liked her coffee. In all the years she'd been with Matt, he'd never once made her coffee. Such a little thing to mean so much, but to Kelly it did. All the effort she'd made, for what? Well, it's over Kelly thought with a sigh of contentment. All's well that ends well. Well, alls well that ends, period.

Sam shuffled into the kitchen and sat at the table looking at Nick cautiously. Nick placed a plate of pancakes and bacon in front of him.

"Eat up Sammy. Water boy is a labor intensive job. You'll need all your energy today."

Nick looked over at Kelly and winked. Sam looked resigned. He shrugged and picked up his fork.

"Well, I guess one game on the sideline is better than three, right?

Nick's team won, by two points. Sam was out of the dog house. Both parents were back from business trips, so Sam was safely ensconced in his own bed for the night. Peggy was dying to ask Kelly what was going on with her and Nick, but couldn't get her alone at the end of the game. Kelly waved goodbye to her family in the parking lot and headed back to the house with Nick.

They spent the rest of the afternoon in bed, leaving only to take Max for a long walk and to pick up Thai food. They stayed up late into the night alternately making love or talking. Kelly tried not to over think about where this was going. She just wanted to live in the moment for once in her life without worrying about it.

On Monday morning at 6:00 am her alarm went off and she padded into the kitchen to make coffee. Nick was already there, sitting on the counter holding out an over sized mug to her.

Kelly smiled at him. "I'm not much of a talker before the first cup of coffee, Nick."

Nick hopped down and pressed Kelly into a hug. He kissed the top of her head and her temple.

"I've got to get to school early today to help out with a few things. I'll see you tonight?"

Kelly nodded and hugged him back. He grabbed his car keys and a travel mug and headed out the front door, locking it from the outside.

Max waited until Nick was gone and pulled a package of bagels off the counter and headed under the table. Kelly sighed, grabbed the almost empty cream cheese tub that Nick had left out for her and threw it under the table.

"Enjoy, you rotten brat. Knock yourself out."

Kelly walked into her mother's warm, fragrant, kitchen with Max in tow. Poppy placed a plate of homemade dog biscuits on the floor for him with a bowl of decaffeinated coffee. Max was happily occupied. Kelly poured herself a large mug of strong coffee and immersed herself in work for the next six hours. Since Thanksgiving things had gotten extremely busy and Carry Prescott was coming in most mornings to help. It was 1:00 o'clock before they took a break, sitting at the pristine kitchen table with a plate of chocolate biscuits and over sized coffee mugs.

Kelly was in a very relaxed, happy mood and Poppy was getting suspicious.

"So Kelly, how was your Sunday evening?"

Kelly shrugged. "Nick and I just hung around and watched TV."

Carry looked from Kelly to Poppy. "Me too, what did you watch?" she asked innocently.

Kelly looked up at Carry and said she didn't remember off the top of her head.

"If I knew there was going to be a quiz, I would have taken notes."

Carry looked a little hurt and was opening her mouth to snap back when she caught the look Kelly was giving her. She quickly closed her mouth, but she was too late.

Poppy stared hard at Kelly.

"Are you and Nick an item now Kelly? Because if that's the case, you need to let Matt know."

Kelly started to protest but Poppy cut her off in mid sentence.

"Boy, will I be glad to see the back side of his mother." All three of them started to laugh.

"Mom! You never told me you didn't like her."

Poppy wiped her eyes with a tissue. "Oh Kelly, what's to like? She's a miserable, bossy old cow. I've never met anyone who didn't think she was a pretentious ass. Just because I didn't vocalize it, doesn't mean I'm an idiot."

Kelly laughed and got up to wash her dishes.

"Yeah, losing a mother- in- law will be the upside of my divorce."

They finished the days work, got all the baked goods ready for the delivery trucks, cleaned, did the prep work for the morning and called it a day, a very long, exhausting day.

Kelly walked into Nick's house to the aroma of something wonderful cooking. Nick was in the kitchen with the table set and wine poured, except he didn't look happy. He had his elbows propped on the table and was staring at Kelly with a resigned expression.

"Matt's mother called. He's in the hospital. He had a car accident and broke a few ribs, his leg and his jaw. He's in and out of consciousness and asking for you. Do you want me to drive you there?"

Twenty minutes later they arrived at the emergency room.

Kay Chambers stood outside Matt's hospital room, presumably as a bouncer, to send the riff raff on their way. Nick walked over and enveloped her in a hug.

"How's he doing, Kay? Any word from the Doctor yet?"

Kay let out a noise that sounded a lot like a sob.

"Well, he's out of the woods, medically speaking, but he's got a long recovery period ahead of him."

Kay glanced at Kelly, giving her the most withering look she was able to conjure up.

"Hopefully, someone who says she loved him and is still technically his wife will make good on her vows, although God only knows why he married her."

Kay shook her head at Nick clearly looking for some acknowledgement at Matt's poor spouse choice. Nick rounded on Kay.

"That's enough, Kay. Stop pretending that Matt's a choir boy. You know way too much to blame this on Kelly."

Kay stared at Nick, aghast.

"Whose friend are you anyway, Nick, because you certainly got here fast enough." She eyeballed them suspiciously. She walked over to the bed side table and grabbed her handbag.

"I'm getting a cup of coffee. Please be gone when I get back, Nick."

With that, Kay took her considerable bulk and headed for the elevator.

Kelly walked into the hospital room and stared at Matt. His leg and arm were set in plaster casts; his face was bruised and swollen. If Kelly didn't know it was Matt, she wouldn't have recognized him.

Matt opened his eyes and saw Kelly. He let out a choking noise and started to cry. Kelly pulled a chair next to the bed and took his hand. He tried to talk to her but his wired jaw and the swelling made him impossible to understand. Kelly shushed him and told him to try to sleep. He nodded his head slightly and was asleep within seconds.

Nick looked at Kelly from the doorway and felt like someone had kicked him in the gut. It was several minutes before Kelly looked up at him, but Nick knew what was coming.

"I have to help him, Nick, you know that, right?"

Nick stared at Kelly and gave her a resigned look.

"I know, Kelly, I know. Just don't count on me being there if you go back to him again." He tossed her the car keys. "I'll catch a cab. Just leave them on the counter when you get home."

Chapter 19

*T*onight was Sam and Peggy's bonding night at the Nutcracker. She'd been so excited to spend the evening together, just the two of them. They were going to see the ballet first, followed by a late night dinner at the Oriental Palace. Peggy's enthusiasm was starting to wane big time though. Sam was not only not excited, he was pissed off that he had to go.

"Mom, the ballet? Really? What if someone sees me?"

Peggy took a deep breath and counted to ten.

"Well, you'll just have to tell them you have the meanest mom on the planet and I forced you to go at gun point."

Sam noticeably perked up.

"That's a great idea, Mom. Thanks."

Peggy tried counting again.

"That's enough, Sam. Just go put your suit on."

Sam nodded agreeably and headed up the stairs. When he came back down, he already had his parka on.

"All set Mom, let's get going."

Peggy smiled. "That's the spirit Sam, you'll see. This is going to be a night you'll remember."

Sam smiled sweetly. "You too, Mom, you too!"

The first half of the play passed quickly. Peggy only had to wake Sam up twice. When they announced intermission, she suggested they get a soda and some Chocolates for the second half. Sam enthusiastically agreed and Peggy headed up the aisle with Sam bringing up the rear. When they walked through the auditorium into the lobby, people started to chuckle and point in Peggy's direction. Puzzled, Peggy turned around to see what they were looking at, and there was Sam, in all his splendor. He had indeed worn his suit pants, but instead of a dress shirt he'd put on an old baseball tee shirt that he'd gotten from The Kenny Ulrich baseball camp. He'd cut the sleeves off and jaggedly cut the bottom so his stomach showed. He'd applied fake tattoos up and down his arms and on his stomach. He looked up at his mother triumphantly. Peggy gave him a little bow and a flourish of her hand in his direction.

"Touché, Sam. Well done."

They stayed for the rest of the show and headed out quickly at the end to avoid the traffic backup.

The Oriental Palace was busy, but they were seated right away. Sam was fascinated with all the Chinese writing on the walls and the colorful pictures. They also had a wall length salt water fish tank that could occupy Sam for hours when he was a toddler. Peggy would spend hours e-mailing her clients while Sam would watch the different fish and leave sticky finger prints all over the glass.

They ordered a poopoo platter, which was Sam's favorite, and drinks, a Roy Roger for Sam and a dry martini for herself. When the food came, Peggy left her untouched drink and Sam who was busy roasting an eggroll on the small open flame in the center of the platter and excused herself to visit the ladies room.

She was reapplying her lipstick when she heard shrieking coming from the direction of their table. She threw her lipstick into her handbag and ran out of the ladies room. Sure enough there were waiters surrounding their table trying to put out the flames that were engulfing the table cloth. Sam ran over and threw his arms around her.

"Mom, I don't know what happened. The flame started to get really big so I threw your drink on it and it kind of exploded."

A waiter walked over to Peggy and Sam and handed them their coats. "You go now. Go!"

Twenty minutes later, they were seated in the diner, eating matzo ball soup and Peggy was laughing so hard she had to keep wiping tears off her face.

"Sam, you are not a dull date, I'll give you that much."

They finished their dinner and ordered a huge, hot fudge sundae which they shared. Peggy couldn't remember the last time she'd had so much fun. Of course, they wouldn't be going back to The Oriental Palace again anytime soon.

Matt was in the hospital for two weeks. Kelly went from work to the hospital, only stopping at home to feed and walk Max. Matt asked if Kelly could stay at the house with him for awhile, until he got back on his feet. She wasn't happy about it but she reasoned that it was the right thing to do.

Kelly tried to talk to Nick about it and explain herself, but he was too angry and disappointed to listen to her. So she had packed her bags and left in a huff.

As she was getting in her car, Nick called out to her from the doorway. "Leave Max with me. You'll be too busy to take care of him and Matt hates him."

Kelly started to argue, realized he was right and let Max out of the car. She mumbled a thank you and drove away feeling deflated.

Kelly slept in the spare bedroom and helped Matt get back and forth to the bathroom. She brought him his breakfast each morning and waited for Kay to arrive before she left for work. Kay made Matt lunch and dinner each day and would leave without talking to Kelly as soon as Kelly was in the door.

With the Christmas rush at work and Matt being so needy, Christmas was here before she was ready to even handle it. She decorated the house, hoping to lift Matt's spirits, but to no avail. He was in a full blown depression and making very slow progress as a result. He'd lost fifteen pounds already and was really having a hard time functioning with the casts and the wired jaw.

Things with Nick were non existent as well. He was busy with mid terms and coaching the wrestling team. He'd also started practices for little league in an indoor facility. When Kelly did come by, he was civil but distant. He was almost acting aloof. If he's doing it to peak my interest, it's definitely working Kelly thought with a sigh. Unfortunately, there's nothing I can do about it right now.

Chapter 20

*W*ith the last of the Christmas orders packaged and on their way to being delivered, Kelly and Poppy opened a bottle of Champagne and sat before Poppy's crackling fire.

Kelly took a small sip of the icy liquid, letting the bubbles linger, savoring the tart taste.

"Here's to our first successful season as partners, sweetheart. You did a fantastic job."

Kelly smiled at her mother.

"Mom, the business was a success before I ever came aboard."

Poppy shrugged. "It might have been successful, but it wasn't fun. Speaking of fun, you'll be here for hors d'oeuvres tomorrow before church? Kay said she was taking Matt to her house until December 26th, so you should be free, right?"

Kelly looked at her mother's hopeful face and agreed to be there Christmas Eve so the whole family could go to the midnight mass together.

When Kelly finally arrived home the house was strangely quiet. Neither, Nick or Max were anywhere to be found. Kelly opened up the refrigerator to pour herself a glass of chilled white wine. Propped up on the bottle was a card with Nick's hand writing. Kelly poured her wine and took the envelope into the living room. After making herself comfortable she opened the card. It was a Christmas card. Nick had put in a snap shot of Max with a Santa hat. Nick's precise hand writing stared up from the page.

"Have a great Christmas, Kelly. I'll miss you. We miss you. I'll be at my parents until New Years Day. They're having their annual New Years Eve party. Please bring your whole family and Jay and Angie. Bring anyone you like as long as it's not a date. That I can't handle. I took Max with me. You're welcome to visit him or take him for Christmas. I just thought the cats could use a good scare."

Kelly laughed and put her head back on the couch. As much as she missed Max, it was nice not to have to take care of someone for a change.

Kelly spent the morning cleaning house. She bagged up clothes for Goodwill, cleaned out the refrigerator, vacuumed, dusted and gave the bathroom a once over. The rest of the day was spent wrapping presents and catching up on her emails. She took her time getting ready for Poppy's. After a long, leisurely bath she polished her toe nails a nice festive red. Poppy had purchased a beautiful dark red cashmere sweater for Kelly to wear, and with nicely cut trousers and strappy gold heels, Kelly was pleased with her appearance. She'd lost about twelve pounds in the last month. With work and taking care of Matt, she just didn't have time to eat.

Kelly pulled her car into her mother's driveway and got her overnight bag out of the trunk and headed up the beautifully decorated walkway. Poppy had strung fairy lights through all the shrubs and along the roof's edge. The inside of the house looked like something out of a story book. Fairy lights, mistletoe and evergreen branches were everywhere. Poppy had placed tea lights on every available surface. She was walking around with a tray of champagne glasses and she hurried over to Kelly when she saw her

come through the door.

"Hello love. I was getting worried. Go put your bag in your room and hurry back. Take a glass of champagne with you. Sam is up to something, so if you can get him to spill the beans, I'd be grateful. Is it too much to ask for one Christmas Eve without the fire department having to be called?"

Kelly laughed and headed up the stairs. She spied Sam whispering to Uncle Mike. Kelly rolled her eyes. Did he learn nothing from operation gnome?

Poppy had outdone herself. Dozens of trays of elegant hors d'oeuvres were passed around by a waiter hired for the evening. Kelly couldn't remember the last time she'd had such a nice relaxed evening. Jay was at his mother's house and promised to come spend the night after they got back from midnight mass. Sam had been on his best behavior for the entire evening.

At 11:15 they all got their coats on and headed to the front door for the five minute ride to church. Poppy opened the front door and let out a shriek and slammed it shut.

"There's a skunk right on the front step" she said, placing her hand on her chest. "How do we get rid of it?"

Kelly went to the living room window and looked out. Sure enough, there was a large skunk sitting front and center.

Peggy sighed. "I think we have to wait for him to move. If we startle him, he'll spray the house and we'll all end up smelling to high heaven for church."

They waited for twenty minutes for Pepe La Pew to move and then Poppy started to get angry.

"What the hell, is he dead? Move it along feller, we've a mass to get to!"

Kelly looked over at Sam who could barely contain his glee. He'd once offered Kelly sixty dollars if she'd let him miss mass. Kelly cracked the front door and took a closer look at the skunk. A little tag was sticking out from underneath his belly. She threw the door open and started to laugh.

"Nice one Sam," she said and bent down to pick up the stuffed animal.

Sam and Uncle Mike were high fiving each other and laughing. Poppy was glaring at the pair of them.

"If we don't get seats at mass because of you two jackasses, heads will roll." Uncle Mike took the stuffed skunk from Kelly..

"No problem Poppy. We'll just bring our little friend here and throw him in the front pews. You'll have a grand seat."

Poppy grabbed the stuffed animal and threw it back down on the porch step.

"That won't be necessary, let's go," Poppy said through gritted teeth.

Within five minutes of mass, Sam was sound asleep. Kelly thought it was a beautiful mass, in spite of Sam drooling on her shoulder.

When they arrived home, they said goodnight to the relatives and Kelly and Poppy settled themselves down in front of the fire with heavily spiked eggnog and Christmas music playing softly in the background.

Kelly dozed off. She woke up with a start when she heard pounding on the back door. She saw Jay waving frantically through the glass sliding door. Kelly hurried over and let him in.

"Oh my God, Kelly. There's a skunk on your front porch that won't move. I've been throwing Skittles at him for the last forty five minutes, and he won't budge!"

Poppy had walked into the kitchen and heard the tail end of Jay's tirade. They both burst out laughing as Jay stared at them bewildered.

"What's so funny?"

Kelly wiped tears from her eyes and poured Jay a scotch. "You can thank Sam for the loss of your Skittles, Jay. Grab some ice from the freezer and join us in the living room."

ew Year's Eve came and went, Kelly couldn't bring herself to attend Nick's parent's party and everyone seemed to have plans, so she spent the night at Peggy's house with Sam and her mother while Peggy and Tim attended a work party. Matt said he wanted to stay home alone and Kelly was tired of trying to cheer him up so she let him have his way. They watched the ball drop and toasted with glasses of sparkling cider.

The months went by quickly and soon spring was in the air. Sam's baseball practices were under way, much to Tim's chagrin.

Tim wanted to kill Peggy. What the hell was she thinking? I haven't played baseball since I was twelve years old, Tim thought furiously. Tim's team had won the state championship that year, which was a huge accomplishment. It was also the reason they'd given him the team so readily.

Tim had wanted to call the league and say there'd been a huge mistake but Sam had already heard through the grapevine that his Dad was the new head coach and he was beside himself with joy. Tim didn't have the heart to tell him he didn't want to do it. Instead he spent time he couldn't spare going over little league rules, studying batting techniques and enlisting help. Nick said he'd give him a hand when he was available since he was the assistant coach for the middle school baseball team.

In desperation, Tim called coach Vinny, his old little league coach. He was hands down the best coach in Rockland but he made Walther Matthau look like Mary Poppins. He smoked in the dugout, drank, and dropped the eff bomb constantly. Politically correct? Not remotely.

Their first game was against the Orioles, the acknowledged best team in the league. The Red Sox played a great game and ended up losing by one run. If their team had been hitting the ball a little better they might have easily won. Still, all of Tim's players were excited that it had been such a close game.

One of the children on the team, Simon Barnes was new to baseball. Naively he said, "Oh well, at least we came in second."

Coach Vinny turned to Simon and gave him his most withering glare.

"Coming in second is like kissing your sister," he sneered. He grabbed Simon's bat and ground his cigarette out on it, then dropped it in the dirt and stalked out of the dugout and left the field without shaking hands with the other team.

Chapter 22

---

*S*ix months had gone by and Angie and Jay were seeing each other on a regular basis. Angie sometimes balked about the agreed upon three times a week minimum, but as their relationship progressed it was more or less just to be ornery. The truth was, she really enjoyed Jay's company.

It was the longest day of work Angie could remember in a very long time. Mark had called in sick and the children were out of sorts and running amok. Peter had once again tried to microwave his I Pad and Levon was moaning at decibel ten. Malik had punched Nakia in the back and pulled her hair. Bobby had urinated in the corner and Stevie had refused to get out of the pool after swimming was over. They were finally able to coax him out of the pool by holding up a sign that said they'd let him have computer time if he got out on his own.

On top of everything else they had given Angie a new teaching assistant who'd never worked with the mentally challenged population before. After twenty minutes she was crying in the bathroom and had to be calmed down. Tyeesha was banging on her desk yelling, "Mommy!"

Nakia lost her mind and yelled "enough" at the top of her lungs.

"I am so frigging sick of this shit!"

Angie glared at her.

Nakia responded, "Oh sure, judge away, Judgerella! I am bringing duct tape in tomorrow and Levon is getting his mouth taped."

Juan stamped his foot. "That is so not cool, Nakia. Levon can't help moaning, it's part of his syndrome!"

Nakia looked at Juan contemptuously. "Why don't you and your floppy hair shut the hell up, Floby?"

Jeannie, Will's one to one counselor shot coffee out of her nose. Angie gasped and looked at Juan who was now breathing heavily through his mouth and looking from face to face, aghast.

Floby was the name they'd secretly given Juan due to his horrible, floppy hair after the Floby Home Hair cutting system that was advertised on late night TV. But for Nakia to tell him was crossing the line.

Juan glared at all of them.

"My hair has been compared to Hugh Grants, you kinky haired bitches! I'm out of here!"

He stormed out, slamming the door behind him. Jeannie looked at Angie in horror, her mouth hanging open. Angie rolled her eyes.

"Oh relax Jeannie, he'll be back. It's his lunch break."

Angie turned to Nakia. "You need to learn to shut you mouth once in awhile. What the heck were you thinking?" Nakia stamped her foot and slapped Angie's desk.

"I was thinking that he's fifteen minutes late every day, doesn't do any work at all, and then has something to say every five minutes. It's enough. Get Floby fired, bitch! There are plenty of people here who want to work so get rid of his sorry ass."

Tyeesha, sensing the tense atmosphere started to jump up and down while punching her bus number into a calculator to show everyone. Malik was standing on a chair trying to press his crotch against the computer. Nakia hauled him off the chair and got a hard pinch for her trouble. Peter was polishing off Angie's coffee and Stevie dropped Juan's phone in the toilet and tried to flush it.

"Alright people, we need to concentrate on the children, not Floby and our apparently kinky hair. Do your jobs," Angie bellowed.

She sat at her desk and proceeded to organize the afternoon lesson she had planned. Just as she was about to call everyone to the work table, Tyeesha slid a calculator in front of her face with her bus number on it. Angie laughed. "No bus today, Tyeesha, you have after school." Tyeesha wailed, turned around and punched Will in the chest. Angie sighed. It was going to be a long day.

Juan came back from lunch looking like the proverbial cat that ate the cream. He was practically jumping up and down with glee.

"Look who I found at the front desk," he said triumphantly.

Jay walked in carrying two large pizza boxes and a bottle of orange soda.

"Who's hungry?" He said with a smile.

Angie tried not to smile back but gave up when she saw how happy the children were. As reluctant as she'd been to admit it, Jay had wormed his way into her heart. He was definitely a keeper, as her Dad was fond of saying. She just couldn't figure out why he wanted her.

Jay was passing out plates of pizza to the children while Nakia fawned all over him, practically drooling and Juan was happily pouring out orange soda, the ugly morning forgotten. Jay even complimented Juan on his hair. Juan turned and glared at Nakia, triumphantly. Nakia choked on her cup of soda and ran for the bathroom. Angie ducked her head down so Juan couldn't see the smile on her face. Really, there was no situation that Jay couldn't fix without even trying.

Angie had been reluctant to tell Kelly about Jay, but Jay had saved her the trouble and opened his big mouth first.

Kelly had called Angie as soon as Jay had left her house. She had been beside herself with mirth. "Oh my God, you two are perfect for each other. I don't know why it never occurred to me before!"

Angie had gotten mad and hung up the phone. Kelly showed up at her house thirty minutes later with coffee for the two of them and donuts for Eddy.

"What is your problem, Angie? This is amazing! Could you please not screw it up for some asinine reason like bad sneakers or dental floss?"

Angie looked at Kelly with a rueful expression. "The thing is Kelly, I've tried to screw it up. It's not possible. Nothing I do pisses Jay off." Angie shook her head woefully. "Why me, Kelly? Why does he think he loves me?"

Kelly laughed and hugged Angie.

"Why not you, Angie? It's about time you found somebody who's as wonderful as you are. And he doesn't think he loves you, he loves you Angie. I've never heard him talk like this before."

Angie squirmed out of the hug and crossed the kitchen to lean on the center island.

"What if I love him back and he figures out I'm not worth it? What then?"

Kelly looked at Angie with sympathy.

"You're just going to have to have a little more faith, Angie. You might not see what the rest of us see in you, but we see it and we love you. Hopefully some day you'll see it too."

In the years that followed college Buddy Longing never once fell off the wagon. He had become the father they hadn't dared to hope for. Eddy worshipped him. They did everything together and Buddy seemed to possess infinite amounts of patience. It took five years before Angie would let herself hope, but her father had long since proved himself, no matter how difficult Bella Longing became. Bella's last visit home, as Angie had started to think of them, had lasted eight months.

Buddy had made sure she'd taken her medicine faithfully, but inevitably the day came when Bella started to show signs of deteriorating.

Buddy had taken her to church. They'd run into Poppy Moriarty on the way in and sat together in the middle of an aisle up front. As soon as Father Paul started his sermon, the topic being "Love thy neighbor," Bella started to laugh uncontrollably. She stood up and much to Poppy's horror yelled out, "Sure, it's ok for you good time Charlie's! Nothing to do but preach and tell us what to do, meanwhile, you've got all the bored women of the parish practically wiping your asses! Good for nothing, good time Charlie's!"

Poppy tried to hide behind her prayer book as Buddy tried to hustle Bella out of the church. Poppy stayed until the end of mass at which point Father Paul pulled her aside for a chat, looking stressed out.

"Now listen Poppy, I know you're a good Catholic, but do you think you could try and convince Buddy to either keep his wife home or maybe change religions?"

Bella Longing's health was failing a little more with each passing year. Angie knew her mother didn't have a lot of time left and she was very grateful to Buddy for making her final days as drama free as possible. If her father could change so dramatically for his family, shouldn't she make the effort to change even a little bit for Jay? Angie decided Jay was worth changing for, too.

Jay walked into his parents' house and helped himself to a seltzer from the fridge. "Anyone home?" he called out. His mother came up the basement stairs with a basket of laundry. Her face lit up when she saw Jay.

"Hi sweetheart. Can I fix you some lunch?"

Jay smiled and looked in the refrigerator. "I got this, Mom, you just sit and fold your laundry."

Jay took out some eggs, a block of cheddar cheese and onions, mushrooms and peppers and started to make two omelets.

Dora Shaw was a large boned woman with an attractive, Nordic looking face and beautiful blue eyes that Jay was lucky enough to inherit. Of her four children, Jay was the one she understood the least. He'd never been into sports. He'd never rough housed with his brothers. She'd honestly assumed he was gay until he'd started dating Angie. When he'd dated girls in the past, it was casual. She had assumed Jay was trying to convince them he was straight. But any idiot could see how wild he was about that Angie. Dora was thrilled with Angie. As her husband Zeb was fond of saying, she's tough enough for both of them.

Jay plated the omelets and sat down across from his mother. They ate in companionable silence for a few minutes while Jay tried to get his thoughts in order.

"Mom," he began cautiously, "how would you feel about helping me pick out an engagement ring for Angie?"

Dora jumped up, dumped her plate in the sink and ran to the closet to put her coat on.

"My handbag is on the counter, honey, let's go."

She couldn't wait to tell her husband. Jay might not care about sports, but as Zeb had stated, "Angie would probably buy any children they had football helmets to wear in the womb!" Jay laughed at his mother's ecstatic face, dumped his plate in the sink with hers and went to pick out Angie's ring.

Matt was on the mend. The casts were off and he was going to physical therapy and working from home. Kelly stayed over a couple of nights a week, but had moved back into Nick's house.

Max was overjoyed to have his mistress back, while Nick seemed indifferent. Kelly was confused as to where they stood, but Nick was so cold that she assumed he was no longer interested. Well, screw you too, buddy, Kelly thought to herself. If he couldn't see that she had to help Matt, then he was an ass.

In the meantime, Matt was begging her to give their marriage another shot. Kelly had no interest, but the guilt was driving her crazy. She'd made it very clear to Matt that their marriage was over, but he seemed to think it was only a matter of time before she came to her senses.

Ten years was a long time. Was she being cold? She wasn't the one who'd cheated. Why should she feel like she owed him? She cleaned his house, did laundry and cooked. As soon as Matt was completely on his feet, as far as she was concerned, he was on his own.

If the tables were turned, there is no way Matt would have done all this for you, Jay would holler at her. Kelly knew he was right, but her being there a few days a week gave Matt a much needed break from Kay. No one should be subjected to Matt's mother seven days a week, not even Matt, Kelly thought with a shudder.

Chapter 23

*A*s the baseball season continued, Sam became noticeably less enthused. All of the children seemed to huddle on one side of the dugout with Coach Vinny smoking on the other side. The children tried to give Coach Vinny a wide berth on the way in and out of the dugout, but he still managed to yell in their faces.

It was a beautiful spring morning and the whole Moriarty family had come out to watch Sam's game. They had set up chairs along the outfield fence. Uncle Mike had even purchased Red Sox tee-shirts for everyone to wear. He'd also brought a megaphone to the game, but Peggy had made him put it in the trunk of his car after he scared the hell out of the center fielder who was two feet away.

Sam had explained to the family that it was an important game according to coach Vinny. A lot would depend on Sam's pitching and Coach Vinny had told him he had better not screw the pooch. Sam was horrified until Kelly explained it just meant don't blow it.

It was the bottom of the fourth inning and Sam was starting to look tired on the pitching mound. He did what Nick had told him to do when he needed a minute to compose himself. He stepped off the mound and walked around it in a circle. Except he was looking a little wild eyed and taking a lot longer than Nick had probably suggested. Kelly suspected it had something to do with the little pep talk Coach Vinny had just given him on the mound. Uncle Mike looked at Kelly nervously. "Kelly, what the hell is he doing pacing around the mound like that? He looks like a dog marking territory, for the love of God. Why doesn't he just pee on the mound and get it over with? He looks like one of them googly eyed bobble head dolls." Tim ran out to the mound and pointed to the kid at third to take over pitching. He told Sam to go and cover third base. Sam was rolling his eyes at Peggy, clearly unhappy.

Uncle Mike yelled out, "Hey Google head cover third and cut the shenanigans!" The new pitcher walked three players in a row, but someone finally hit a pop up and the inning was over.

When Sam got back in the dugout Coach Vinny told him to put on a dress. Tim told Vinny to tone it down. Vinny got in Tim's face and said maybe they both needed dresses.

In the meantime, the other team loaded up the bases. Sam came up to the plate with bases loaded and two outs. The pitcher was throwing right down the middle. With a 3-0 count, coach Vinny told the child on third to steal home. The only problem was that it was the slowest boy in the league, Wyatt Thompson. By the time he reached home plate, the catcher had been waiting with the ball to tag him out for two full minutes. Sam watched the whole episode transpire in horror. He stalked into the dugout, packed his baseball bag up and left the dugout. His team went out onto the field as Coach Vinny screamed for Sam to get his ass to third base. When he didn't, he sent another child to cover Sam's position.

It was a quick inning and Kelly and Peggy spotted Sam outside the dugout just as the announcer, Jay called out, "And now at bat, Sammy the bull." When Sam didn't appear behind home plate he called out, "Where's Sam? Oh, there he is, behind the dugout. Why is Sam behind the dugout?" Kelly and Peggy ran as fast as they could to try and do damage control. Peggy turned to Kelly.

"Oh my God, it sounds like Where's Waldo, right?"

Sam saw them coming and called out, "Ok, I've had enough. Coach Vinny is an idiot, let's go."

Kelly hissed at Sam through her teeth, "Sammy, get back in there and bat."

Sam shook his head adamantly. "I can't take anymore. I'm going to need a lot of therapy because of this season, let's go!"

It cost Peggy a trip to the ice cream store after the game, but they were able to coax Sam back into the dugout and up to the plate. It was the bottom of the sixth inning and Sam cracked one to right field and slid into second. The next boy at bat struck out, followed by the next batter who didn't even swing. The last boy at bat, Marco Tamarro crushed the ball and slid into third, safe by three feet. The umpire, who had clearly had enough of Coach Vinny as well, yelled, "You're out!"

The parents went crazy. Uncle Mike started to bellow, "Cheaters" at the top of his lungs. Kelly called him on his cell phone to try and get him to stop yelling and he ignored her calls until the fifth one, at which point he yelled across the field, "I know, Kelly. You want me to stop yelling and shut up! I get it, now stop calling me!"

With that he resumed yelling "cheater" at the umpire.

Coach Vinny went out and kicked dirt on the umpire's feet, at which point Uncle Mike stopped yelling at the umpire and started to yell, "you're a gobshite" at Coach Vinny.

All the parents were going into the dugout and packing up their children's belongings and hustling them out of there and into the parking lot as quickly as they could. Kelly called Nick's cell phone.

"Hi Nick, this is Kelly. I think you need to step in and take over for Coach Vinny before Tim get's lynched and Uncle Mike gets shot. You don't have to talk to me but Sam really needs you."

Tim called a parents meeting for the team for first thing Saturday morning to try and downplay the damage done by Coach Vinny. Everyone showed up with the exception of the Doyle family who hadn't shown up for the last four games anyway.

Tim apologized profusely for unwittingly unleashing Coach Vinny on their children and introduced Nick as the new head coach. He listed Nick's credentials. The parents tried not to look skeptical, after all, most of them had already met Nick on numerous occasions and liked him, but after Vinny, none of them were too sure whether Tim's judgment could be trusted.

One impeccably groomed mother raised her hand and Tim nodded at her to go ahead and speak.

"So we can be reasonably assured Coach Nick won't kick our children in the ass when they strike out or make them wear a sign that says "I pee sitting down" when they make an error?"

Tim coughed and looked uncomfortably around at the assembled parents.

"Um, just for the record, no one actually wore that sign. I threw it out as soon as I saw him try to put it on your son. I'm very sorry, Tina. No, with Nick at the helm you can rest assure that sort of thing will never happen."

Nick raised his hand and invited the parents to rotate helping out in the dugout so they could gauge his coaching ability for themselves. He told them if they weren't happy he'd step aside immediately. This seemed to appease everyone. After all, Coach Vinny never let any parent within a five foot radius of the dugout. If they even tried to hand a bottle of water in to their child during the game, he'd been known to spit chewing tobacco at the hapless parent.

The rest of the baseball season went by without a hitch. The only real problem being that the more Nick helped out, the less Tim seemed to be around. He showed up for fewer games and no practices. Sam seemed fine with it, but Peggy was furious.

It all came to a head at the end of May. Tim was busy packing for yet another business trip when Peggy confronted him. She tried to explain that he was losing his family, but Tim was too preoccupied to even listen. He finished packing, closed his suitcase and headed towards the front door. Peggy followed him outside where a town car was waiting to take him to the airport. She literally blocked his path.

"Tim, I need you to listen to what I have to say, I need you to hear me for a change."

Something about the timbre of Peggy's voice pulled Tim up short and he looked down at her upturned face.

"I want you to move out when you come back from your business trip. I refuse to do this anymore. I can't. I'm done. You can see Sam whenever you want, but I want you out."

Tim opened his mouth to speak, but closed it when he realized he didn't have a clue what he wanted to say. He put his bag in the cars trunk and climbed into the backseat and rolled the window down.

"Just give me a couple of weeks to find an apartment close by and I'll have a moving company pick up my things. Let me know what days are ok for me to have Sam.

I don't want this to get ugly, Peggy. I'll do whatever you want."

Peggy nodded, trying to blink back tears. She waved goodbye and walked quickly up the porch steps and into the house.

She went to the kitchen and walked into the huge pantry, closing and locking the doors behind her. She slid down the wall until she was sitting on the tile floor and spent the next twenty minutes sobbing. When Peggy finally stopped crying she felt drained, but also relieved, like a weight was lifted from her shoulders.

She went to the kitchen sink and splashed cold water on her face. Sam was absorbed with Xbox until they had to leave for his afternoon baseball game so she had the morning free. It was time for some coffee and homemade blueberry muffins that her Mom had dropped off. Followed by yoga, of course!

Kelly had the morning off and it was a gorgeous day. She grabbed Max's leash and water dish and headed to Rockland Lake State Park to spend some quality time hiking with her dog.

Sam and Peggy were already there with their bicycles. Peggy had explained that Sam had been playing Xbox and screaming at his Madden players when she'd finally had enough and turned the TV off and forced him to come to Rockland Lake with her. Mother and son seemed to be having a great time together so it had turned out to be a wise decision. They had passed her twice when Kelly decided to sit at a picnic table for a few minutes and let Max chase geese to his hearts content. Kelly tilted her head back and let the sun wash over her upturned face. It really was a perfect day. Not too hot, with a little breeze.

Bill Camden spotted Max by the waters edge and turned and scanned the picnic tables looking for Kelly.

Her eyes were closed and she opened them when she heard someone walking towards her.

"Hey Kelly, how are you? It's great to see you! I see you brought Max along for protection."

Kelly laughed as they turned to watch Max, who was in the process of getting chased around by an irate duck who hadn't appreciated getting his butt sniffed..

"Yeah, he's a real toughie alright, Bill."

Bill sat down on the park bench with Kelly and sighed. "How's Matt doing? Are you two back together?"

Kelly shook her head. "Nah, I think it's time we both moved on, Bill. I just don't trust him."

Bill smiled "Well at least you won't have to fight over Max, Matt hates him." Kelly nodded in agreement. "Yes, he does, but you never know with Matt. He can be very vindictive. He'll probably try and get joint Max custody just to drive me crazy."

Bill stared at Kelly thoughtfully, deciding what he wanted to say.

"Well, I don't think he'll get anywhere with that, Kelly. Nick has all the paper work, since he's the one who bought Max for you in the first place."

Kelly stared at Bill, her eyes widening in surprise. Then she laughed sadly.

"I should have known Matt would never do something that wonderful for me." Bill dropped his head onto his hands which were propped on his knees.

"Nick wanted you to be happy. He knew Matt was cheating from the beginning, Kelly. We told him to mind his own business, that Matt would get his act together. Even when it was obvious he wouldn't stop fooling around, we told Nick you'd hate him for being the messenger. I told him his feelings for you were clouding his judgment. I'm so sorry Kelly. I wish we had all told you. Nick's loved you since college.

Matt just couldn't let him have you. Like you said, he's a vindictive bastard. He knew Nick loved you and no way would he let Nick have an opportunity to tell you."

Kelly looked like she'd been sucker punched. "All this time, why didn't Nick just tell me?"

Bill gaped at Kelly. "Of course he told you Kelly, you just weren't listening." Kelly hugged Bill and stood up.

"I need to go talk to Matt, Bill. Once I clean up that mess, I hope Nick will forgive me for not paying attention. I hope I didn't blow it."

Bill laughed. "Trust me Kelly, better late than never. Go talk to him, he's waited this long, I'm sure he'll listen. But first let's save Max from that duck!"

Kelly pulled into Matt's driveway. She couldn't get over the fact that he'd never fessed up about Max. She should have known he would never have bought Max. She obviously hadn't wanted to see it. Some of her anger at Matt had dissipated on the ride over. Matt was never a great husband. Her own willingness to ignore it had caused her to waste way too many years.

Kelly used her key to let herself in, not bothering to knock or ring the bell. None of her belongings were here, so basically all she needed to do was say goodbye and leave her key. Whatever happened with Nick, Kelly knew for sure she would never go back to

Matt.

Kelly heard moaning coming from the bedroom. Her first thought was that Matt had fallen out of bed and reinjured himself. Alarmed, she ran to the bedroom and threw the door open. Matt and his physical therapist were having sex, and judging from the position they were in, Matt's injuries were no longer an issue. Kelly just stood there in shock. Matt jumped up, sending Susan the therapist flying off the bed.

"Kelly, don't jump to conclusions."

Kelly started to laugh uncontrollably. "Matt," she said, trying to stop the laughter long enough to get the words out, "I just came by to drop my key off. There's no way we're getting back together."

She looked at Susan. "Good luck with this one. I hope he's worth all the effort you're putting into him. Oh, and by the way Matt, I know about Max so don't even think about pretending you want to see him."

Matt's face took on an ugly look.

"Oh, so Nick finally told you, huh?"

Kelly looked at Matt sadly. "This was never really about you and me, was it? You hate Nick that much?"

Matt looked at Kelly angrily.

"Don't worry, Matt. Your secret's safe with me."

Kelly turned and walked out of the house they'd shared together for the last time. Closing the door behind her, Kelly felt so relieved she wanted to jump for joy.

As she was walking to her car Matt's mother pulled into the driveway and hauled her massive frame from out of her Lincoln town car.

"Why, what a nice surprise, the doting wife. It's so wonderful of you to make an appearance,", Kay said sarcastically. "I hope you didn't upset Matt. He doesn't need your nonsense right now, Lady Jane."

Kelly gave Kay her most sympathetic and concerned look.

"You are so right, Kay. I think he's in a lot of pain today. The doors open. He's in the bedroom. I think you should go straight in and offer your assistance."

Kay brushed past Kelly and waddled up the steps as quickly as her bulk would allow.

Kelly drove to Nick's house and let Max out into the fenced back yard, where he could happily chase small animals and lay down comfortably in the shade. Kelly checked to make sure his water dish was full and then headed inside to take a shower. She got dressed with care, putting on a casual sundress that made her look tall and thin. She blew her hair out so that it tumbled down her back in soft waves and applied mascara and lip gloss with a light hand. When she was finished she checked out her reflection in the full length bathroom mirror and decided she looked pretty good, if she said so herself. She only hoped Nick would think so too.

Kelly nervously made her way into the stands and sat with Peggy to watch Sam's game. Kelly looked at her sister. Peggy looked tired and her face was puffy.

"Is everything ok, Peggy?" Peggy shook her head and coughed into her hand.

"I asked Tim to leave, Kelly. I'm tired of pretending. He's made no effort in years."

Kelly put her arm around her sister's shoulders.

"I'm really sorry. I'm here if you need me." Peggy smiled sadly at her younger sister.

"I know that Kelly, you always are. You've never let me down and I don't thank you enough for it. I don't know what I'd do without you."

They sat companionably and watched Sam's game. All the children seemed happy to be there, which was a vast improvement from Coach Vinny's reign of terror. Nick looked so handsome with his baseball shirt and team hat on. He had a pre summer tan from being outside so much and he looked like he was having fun. Even when he argued a call, he did it in a nonoffensive way that had the umpires laughing. Nick would throw his hands in the air and laugh, as if to say, "Hey, I gave it a shot."

Nick kept scanning the bleachers and Kelly hoped he'd seen her sitting with Peggy. Just as Kelly was working up the nerve to go down to the fence and say hello between innings, Nick looked up, smiled and waved. Kelly started to wave back when she realized Nick wasn't waving to her, he was waving to the gorgeous brunette who had just arrived and sat four rows up and directly in back of Kelly. Peggy watched as Kelly's face fell.

"She looks very young, Kelly, maybe she's just a student and Nick is being friendly?"

Kelly looked at her sister and rolled her eyes. They watched the rest of the game in silence, only cheering when Sam got up to bat or made a play in the field, both of them feeling too tired and depressed to make the effort for anyone else's child.

After the game Kelly hugged Peggy and said she'd meet her at Poppy's house, then she high tailed it out of there. No way was she being introduced to Nick's date. Peggy waited with the other mothers as their children got their bags packed up and went out to right field for their after game pep talk. They'd won by two runs so with any luck it should be a short one.

The attractive brunette came to stand with the waiting parents and one of the nosier Moms introduced herself. The girls name was Cara. Brody's mom, Ellen looked the poor girl up and down frostily before asking in a bitchy tone, "So, how long have you and Nick been dating because, no offense, you look a little on the young side." Cara started to laugh and Ellen looked even more pissed off.

"We're not dating! He's my Uncle. I'm Uncle Nick's oldest brother's daughter. I'm here visiting for the week because my aunt is taking me to look at colleges!"

Peggy jumped up and down and clapped, causing the other mothers to look at her strangely. She ran to the fence and called out to Nick.

"Nick, something's come up and I've got to run. Could you drop Sam to Poppy's house when you're finished?"

Nick nodded yes and waved Peggy off so he could wrap up his talk and let the new teams take the field. Peggy called Kelly's cell phone but it went directly to voice mail. She tried Poppy's home phone and got the answering machine. She raced over to her mother's house, but there were no cars in the driveway. Peggy let herself in and poured herself a huge mug of her mother's fragrant coffee. She sat down to wait for Sam.

Nick pulled up ten minutes later and Peggy waved goodbye as Nick backed out of the driveway after dropping Sam off. His niece followed behind in her own car. Peggy went back in to make Sam a snack. Oh boy, she thought. I hope Kelly listens to her voice mail.

Kelly was in the process of packing a suitcase. No way in hell was she going to watch Nick and his new girlfriend cuddle on the couch, or even worse, lock themselves in the bedroom.

Max spotted the suitcase and went into full fledged canine panic, blocking the door and wrapping his paws around Kelly's legs. She wasn't getting out of the house without Max, that was for sure.

She finished packing a bag with three days worth of clothes. She'd come and pack up the rest of her belongings when Nick was at work. She rolled her suitcase into the hallway just as Nick and his girlfriend walked in.

Kelly rudely walked past them, bumping Nick with her suitcase and dumped it by the front door. She then stalked past them into the kitchen to retrieve her pocketbook.

Nick angrily followed her into the kitchen.

"What the hell was that all about, Kelly?"

Kelly gave Nick the most withering look she could muster.

"Do whatever you want with your very young tramp, but I'm not hanging around to watch or listen."

Nick looked at Kelly's angry face and his face broke into a huge smile.

"Wow. If I knew bringing my niece here would drive you wild with jealousy, I would have done it months ago."

Nick crossed the kitchen and wrapped his arms around Kelly, kissing her passionately. He broke the kiss and looked her in the eyes.

"I've missed you so much, Kelly."

Kelly started to cry. "I thought I blew it. I thought you were over me."

Nick laughed. "Oh, I plan to be over you, Kelly. Over, under, sideways, you're never getting rid of me."

Cara cleared her throat loudly in the kitchen doorway.

"Hello, I can hear you guys? Uncle Nick, I'm going back to the house to have dinner with your parents. I'll tell them you had a baseball emergency."

Cara chuckled and left the house before Nick could respond. Nick picked Kelly up and threw her over his shoulder.

"I have some matters that need to be discussed in the bedroom, Kelly. I hope you haven't made any plans for the next two or three days."

Chapter 24

*J*ay paced nervously back and forth. He had everything planned out. He'd bought champagne. He
had the ring and it was a beauty. A big, square diamond
surrounded by rubies, set in platinum. He just wasn't sure
what Angie's answer would be. He'd chosen a Yankee
game to ask for Angie's hand in marriage, but he'd do it
quietly. He knew if he did it on the billboard the first
thing America would see was his new fiancé punch him in
the face. Except, once they were there watching the game,
he couldn't bring himself to ask. He'd rather everything
stay the same as it was right now than force Angie's hand
and have her dump him.

A week went by and Jay still couldn't think of a way to
ask that would guarantee a positive outcome. He couldn't
think of some magical way that would ensure Angie would
be beside herself with joy and not stalk out of the house
and change her phone number.

It finally came to a head three weeks later when they
were sitting on the couch companionably eating Jay's
home made barbecue lime wings and mocking the contes-
tants on "Bachelor Pad." Angie laughed out loud when
one of the women admitted she was pining for Brad who
was clearly gay.

"Wake up bitch! He wants Matt, not you!"

Jay blurted out "Marry me, Angie" before he had time to chicken out.

Angie rolled her eyes, got up and left the room. Jay dropped his head into his hands. What was I thinking, he berated himself.

Angie came back into the room carrying a bottle of pink champagne and two crystal, fluted glasses. She placed them on the table and then dropped to her knees in front of Jay. She reached into her shirt and pulled the engagement ring box out and handed it to Jay.

"Try again Jay, this time the way you planned it."

Jay stared at Angie with his mouth hanging open.

"You are a total bitch."

He pulled Angie up, dropped to one knee, took the ring out of the box and stared up at her.

"Angie, I love you with my whole heart. Marry me. Anyone else will kill your ass. I am the only one who really gets how wonderful you are."

Angie tried the ring on.

"Wow, diamonds, and rubies. I guess your Mom helped you pick it out?"

Jay opened the champagne and poured two glasses.

"So, what's your answer Angie? Are we toasting our engagement or am I dumping them over your head?"

Angie grabbed a flute.

"Yes. My answer is yes, Jay. I love you."

Staring into his eyes Angie took her expensive glass of champagne and proceeded to dump it over her fiancés head.

Angie opened Jay's blog the next day and laughed out loud.

"Finally! Maybe now the philanderer will get all the free "physical therapy" he can handle. Three strikes and you're out buddy. Caught red handed again. The baseball coach wins in the game of love. Speaking of love, what single, sexy, heterosexual (that part is for you, Dad) gossip columnist finally talked his feisty little psycho of a girlfriend into tying the knot? And I didn't even need the photo shopped pictures of her with the farm animals!"

wo months passed and life was better. Now that Tim was no longer living in the house, Peggy felt as if a heavy burden had been lifted off of her chest. She didn't feel angry all the time. She was still doing all the housework and cooking, but she no longer had to step over Tim to do it. Sometimes, in the evening she was a little lonely, but she was ok with that for now. Even Sam was more relaxed. As much as he might miss Tim living under the same roof, he really didn't miss the tension that was like thick smog weighing the house down.

Oddly enough, now that Tim wasn't living with them, he was transforming into super Dad. He took Sam every other weekend and at least twice a week. He paid attention to Sam, no longer spending all his time on the phone or his lap top. Sam looked forward to spending time with Tim, excited about whatever father/son type activity Tim had planned for them.

It was a Friday evening and Sam was waiting for his father to pick him up for the weekend. They were going to see the new "Avengers" movie and Sam was really excited. Peggy was so grateful that Tim was making time for Sam consistently. Sam was genuinely happy.

The doorbell rang and Sam ran over and threw the door open. Tim was on the other side, freshly showered and shaved, wearing a polo shirt and jeans. He handed some yellow roses to Sam.

"Hey Sammy, are you ready to go? Why don't you give these to your mom and put your bag in the car and I'll be right with you."

Sam ran and handed the flowers to Peggy with a big smile on his face. He threw his arms around her and kissed and hugged her. Peggy hugged him tightly and kissed his head.

"I'll see you on Sunday, Mom. Have fun with Aunt Kelly."

Sam grabbed his bag and ran out to the car to put it into the back seat. Peggy smiled at Tim.

"Have a good time at the movie. He's been looking forward to it all week."

Tim hesitated in the doorway and turned back to look at Peggy.

"It's great to see you, Peggy."

Tim turned to leave, stopped and turned to look at Peggy again. He raked his hands through his hair, making it stand on end, a nervous tick that Sam copied to a tee. He cleared his throat.

"Any chance you could cancel with Kelly and come to dinner and a movie with us?"

Peggy started to shake her head no. Tim pulled the tickets out of his back pocket to show Peggy he'd bought three.

"I got an extra just on the off chance you'd say yes."

Peggy hesitated. "Tim, this is your time with Sam. I don't want to intrude."

Tim started to plead his case when Sam stuck his head in the doorway.

"Please Mom, just the three of us?"

Peggy looked at Sam's hopeful face and sighed. "Are you sure it's ok, Tim?"

A huge smile lit Tim's face up.

"Its not ok, Peggy, it's great!"

Matt was furious. Nick had the girl, the money, even the damn dog.

"Honey, come and eat."

Matt sighed. He'd been seeing Susan for a couple of months now and two days ago she'd dropped the bombshell that she was pregnant and it was his. She'd looked at him with her dull brown eyes brimming with tears, all hopeful, like she had given him such wonderful news. He'd been just about to tell her he'd put in for a day off the following week to take her for an abortion when she blurted out, "I told your mother already. She's so excited."

Matt had stared at Susan in horrified shock. Maybe her eyes weren't so dull after all. He had clearly underestimated her.

Sam sat next to his mom during the movie, making sure that his parents sat next to each other. He watched out of the corner of his eye as Tim casually reached for Peggy's hand. When his Mom didn't pull it away from him, Sam sank down in his seat with a sigh. It was a start, he thought happily.

Chapter 26

It was February, but you wouldn't know it where they were, Sam thought. He stared around and tried to take in all the beautiful sights. The blue green water and white sugar sand were incredible. It might look like sugar, but it sure didn't taste like it. He knew he shouldn't have listened to Uncle Mike. The weather was perfect, the sun was setting pink and orange over the water and his whole family was here, even Max! Aunt Kelly and Nick had opted for a destination wedding in Saint Lucia. Aunt Kelly looked stunning in a simple, white silk halter dress that fell in soft waves to the sand. She was barefoot and her hair was pulled off her face and tumbled down her back in soft waves. Nick looked handsome in a lightweight tan suit with a white shirt and white silk tie. His Mom, Aunt Angie, Maureen, and Grandma Poppy wore similar dresses to Aunt Kelly's, but theirs were a light teal color. Sam and his dad, Jay, and Bill were wearing the same suit as Nick, but with light teal ties. Everyone was barefoot. Sam couldn't get over the fact that no one had to wear shoes. How great was that!

It was a very relaxed atmosphere, but even so, Sam was nervous. He was the ring bearer after all, and that was a big responsibility.

As they said their vows and he handed Nick the ring, Sam turned and looked for his parents. They were happily staring at each other.

Angie and Jay were getting married in three months and Sam was their ring bearer also, as long as he didn't royally screw up Kelly's wedding. Angie had told him to be on his best behavior or she'd kick his butt from here to China. He glanced at her nervously. Angie was having a backyard wedding. Jay's parents were even going to roast a pig.

Uncle Mike and Aunt Danis waved to Sam and gave him the thumbs up sign. Operation ring had gone off without a hitch. Soon it would be time for Uncle Mike's big surprise. He had gotten a ton of fireworks and they were going to surprise everyone when the sun went down. Sam hoped operation fireworks went off better than operation gnome had. Oh well, they'd find out soon.

Jay's column the following day read as follows,

"What beautiful bride masquerading as a pastry queen married her silver spooned middle school teacher on the white sands of St. Lucia last night? The fireworks were flying as they danced into the wee hours of the morning. Not even the accidental gazebo fire that was caused by a misfired firework could put a damper on the festivities! All's well that ends well, folks!"

CPSIA information can be obtained at www.ICGtesting.com
Printed in the USA
BVOW02s1645230713

326603BV00001B/8/P

9 781457 519499